PUBLISHING

**Based on the Hallmark Channel Original Movie**

Leigh Duncan

www.hallmarkpublishing.com
For more about the movie visit:
www.hallmarkchannel.com/a-country-wedding

# Table of Contents

# Chapter One

B radley Suttons twirled his Stetson on the tips of his fingers. Light glinted off the buckle on the fourteen-hundred-dollar hat that had been a gift from his agent. In the shadows beyond the cameras that tracked his every move, someone made a chopping motion, meaning *Stop that*.

Bradley stilled. He traced his fingers over the brim and gave himself a stern reminder to keep his trademark smile in place while he willed away the urge to squint or squirm or stand and walk straight out of the studio.

*Quit your bellyaching.* He wasn't really going to complain about the dizzying heat or the blinding glow that came from all the spotlights aimed at him, was he? Not when he'd spent the past ten years working to get where he was. Every step he'd taken, every stage he'd stepped onto in the bars around Nashville, every mic he'd poured his heart and soul into—they'd all led to this moment.

He glanced at the incredibly talented, beautiful

woman seated next to him on the couch. Catherine tipped her head toward his. The smile she always wore in public, the one that rarely touched eyes the color of fine cognac, deepened as she met his gaze. A long, blond curl slid over her shoulder. Bradley's fingers ached to reach out, tuck the errant hair back into place. Aware that millions of viewers were watching, he merely cupped his knee. He was a lucky, lucky man. He'd landed the girl of his dreams, signed a recording contract, amassed a fortune, and now, finally, had the fame that guaranteed the fulfillment of his every wish. Not too bad for a kid whose whole world had come tumbling down around him at thirteen.

The final chorus of "Love Don't Die Easy" bounced off the walls of the studio. He looked up as the hit that had catapulted him into stardom came to an end.

"I love that song." The host of the nation's most popular morning talk show tapped his fingers on the armrest of his chair. Seated to give viewers the full benefit of the panoramic view of Hollywood over his shoulder, Stan beamed a dreamy smile straight into the cameras. "How did it feel to win Album Of The Year at the Grammys?"

*Surreal.* Bradley glanced down at the toes of his shoes. The Italian leather boots probably cost more than he'd earned in the entire year he'd written that song. He leaned forward, directing his answer at the blinking red light on Camera Three rather than their host, just like Catherine had coached him to do. "Well, not too long ago I was playing in bars and clubs around Nashville. So, winning a Grammy has been quite a change." Thanks to the award, he had the life that, a few years ago, he'd only dreamed of living.

Not that everything was perfect. All the newfound fame and fortune had placed so many extra demands on his time that he was way behind on the new album. Between his schedule and Catherine's work on what was sure to be another blockbuster movie, the two of them rarely spent any time alone together. When she'd called last night and asked if he could free up his morning, he'd had a momentary vision of the two of them eating breakfast and trading kisses over orange juice and coffee. Instead, they'd spent the last two hours in makeup and rehearsals before they were ushered onto the set.

But no one turned down the opportunity to appear on Stan's show. No one. Not unless they wanted to watch their careers sink below the horizon like the setting sun. Careful not to let even the slightest hint of frustration show, Bradley eased back into the plush leather couch when the host's attention shifted.

"Catherine Mann." Stan's dark eyes lit with the fervor of a true fan. The coppery brackets around his mouth deepened as, exuding confidence and poise, he crossed one long leg over the other. "It's a real thrill to have you in the studio today."

"Thank you, Stan." Catherine's perfectly modulated voice caressed the mics while she gave the shy smile that had first delighted movie goers when she was a child, turned her name into a household word as a teen, and stolen his heart the moment Bradley had met her. "It's a pleasure to be here."

"You discovered Bradley, didn't you?" The consummate morning show host, Stan dove straight into the meat of the interview. "I mean, he was already well known in Nashville. But you brought him to Los Angeles and got him a recording deal."

Bradley felt his shoulders stiffen. Sure, things had begun to change for him once he and Catherine had started seeing each other. Her name had opened a few doors. But it had been his talent that had propelled him upward and gotten him where he was today.

"I introduced him to a few people," Catherine admitted. She slipped her perfectly manicured fingers over his knee and stared deeply into his eyes. "But he's a pretty talented guy. He got himself a recording deal."

Her firm answer shut down Stan's line of questioning and soothed the acidic burn in Bradley's stomach. Undaunted, the talk show host smoothly changed subjects. "And the two of you have been inseparable ever since?"

The melodic tones of Catherine's laugh echoed through the small space. "I think the first time I heard Bradley sing"—emotion flickered in her eyes for an all-too-brief moment before she turned to face Stan—"I fell in love with him."

As if he sensed a story, Stan leaned forward. "Are you saying the two of you might have some news for us one day?"

Bradley straightened and said, "We like to keep our

private lives private." In rehearsals, Stan had offered repeated assurances that his guests' personal lives would remain off-limits. Yet less than five minutes into the interview, the host was already prying into matters Bradley and Catherine had decided they'd rather not have aired on national TV. He looked to Catherine for support.

"We're engaged to be married," his bride-to-be blurted.

Despite the countless stage appearances and a thousand-and-one coaching sessions where he'd learned to keep a carefully crafted façade in place, Bradley couldn't even begin to hide his surprise.

He and Catherine had talked about this. They'd decided to keep the depth of their feelings for one another hidden from their adoring—but demanding—fans who'd insist on knowing every detail of their wedding plans. She knew how important it was to him to keep their relationship to themselves. So why had she just shared the news of their engagement on national TV?

"Now, I know we agreed not to share this publicly, but..." Catherine patted his arm. The wattage on her signature smile increased to the point where it practically guaranteed to turn her fans' hearts all aflutter. "I just want the whole world to know how happy I am."

"Well, you heard it here first, folks." Stan's pleased grin announced to viewers everywhere that he'd just scored the scoop of the century. "Catherine Mann and Bradley Suttons are engaged to be married!"

Bradley took a deep breath, steadied his nerves, and aimed a loving look at his fiancée. There really wasn't anything else for him to do, was there? He couldn't very well shut the door now that the horse had already bolted out of the barn. Besides, if he knew anything about his fiancée, it was that Catherine never made a move in public without having a very good reason for it.

Now, he just needed to figure out what that reason was.

Sarah Standor dusted her hands on the back of her well-worn jeans as the screened door she'd been walking in and out of her entire life swung shut behind her. Voices came from the corner of the roomy ranch house. She'd left the TV on to keep her rescue dogs company while she fed and watered the horses this morning. When she glanced at the screen, her footsteps slowed.

The devastatingly handsome cowboy on the talk show sat next to Catherine Mann, America's reigning box-office queen. Sarah resumed her march to the coffeemaker and poured herself a much-needed cup. The starlet on TV giggled like a schoolgirl, tossed her long blonde curls, and announced their engagement. The groom-to-be looked as if he'd just swallowed a canary.

Sarah shook her head and laughed. *Bradley Suttons.* Along with every other person who lived within a fifty-mile radius, she'd followed the meteoric rise of Mill

Town's favorite son. It didn't seem to matter to anyone that Bradley had moved clear across the country when he was thirteen and never once returned for a visit. Or that the house he'd lived in as a child had sat vacant all these years. The good citizens of the town and surrounding areas had claimed him as their own, and that was that.

And now, he was engaged to be married to Catherine Mann, America's sweetheart. Talk about power couples. Their union was sure to top all the Who's Who lists from Nashville to Hollywood, and everywhere in between.

"Well, congratulations, Brad-Bird." Sarah smiled.

A noise from the other end of the house interrupted before she'd finished doctoring her coffee with cream and sugar. She glanced down the hallway that ran as straight as a shotgun from the back door to the front of the house. A familiar figure stood on the wide porch. Sarah noted the suit and tie the banker wore beneath his Stetson and sighed. She'd hoped to put off the inevitable just a little while longer, but it looked like the day she'd been dreading had arrived. Forcing a cheery note into her voice, she called, "Mornin' James."

"Mornin'." Without waiting for an invitation, James let himself in.

"What brings you out here so early?" Sarah took a steadying breath and prepared for the worst. She'd known she couldn't dodge the banker forever. In a place the size of Mill Town, there really wasn't anywhere to hide.

"Well, I had to come out here to see you since you won't answer any of my phone calls or emails." His boot heels rattling against the hardwood floors, James swept the wide-brimmed hat from his head and ran a hand over his sparse hair.

Sarah propped one hand on the kitchen table and leaned on it for support. She was pretty sure she was going to need it. Still, it wouldn't do to let the banker see her sweat. Not quite sure how she did it, she managed a teasing smile. "Well, I don't got time for phone calls and emails. I got a ranch to run." Hoping she'd guessed wrong about her visitor's intentions, she asked, "How's your mama?"

"She's...she's real good." His expression far too serious for a social call, James moved closer.

"She get those garden roses I sent over?" It really was a shame that her boarding stables didn't produce revenue as well as her flowers did. When it came to those, she was known throughout the county for her green thumb. She grabbed the remote control and turned down the volume on the television set.

"She did, and I thank you." James rocked his hat back and forth, talking with his Stetson like people back East spoke with their hands.

"She is such a sweet lady." Uncertain how much longer she could stall, Sarah sipped from her mug. "James, you want some coffee?"

"I'd love a half a cup of coffee." James parked his

hat on the kitchen table. He rubbed one finger down his equine nose and straightened the strings of his bolo tie. "But you need to quit changing the subject, 'cause we need to talk about your finances."

Sarah heard the frustration in his voice. It pained her to put her friend in such an awkward spot, but what else was she supposed to do?

She'd grown up in this house. She knew every creaking floorboard. She knew the way to twist the handle in the shower to coax the most hot water from the ancient boiler, and that she could cool the entire house by propping open the front and back doors on a summer's evening.

Still, even though the ranch had been in her family for generations, she could've walked away from it if she only had herself to think about. But there was far more to it than that. If she lost the ranch, what would become of the horses she cared for? Of the dogs she'd rescued and who now served as her surrogate family? Who would tend to the gardens that provided flowers for weddings and funerals and high school proms and, yes, brought such joy to people like James's mother?

She couldn't lose the ranch. She just couldn't. The ugly fact was, though, she didn't have the money to pay off all her debts.

Hoping to stall, she resorted to the one thing that had worked so far—she hedged. "Now, my mama told me never to talk about politics or money in mixed company," she said as she poured James's coffee and topped off her own cup.

"There's no getting around this, Sarah." James held out his empty palms. "I'm going to have to foreclose on you and sell off this ranch if you can't find a way to make the mortgage payments. If it were up to me—"

"It is up to you, Jimmy." With more firmness than she'd intended, she handed him his cup. "You're the president of Mill Town Bank."

James's voice rose in protest. "I don't *own* the bank, Sarah."

Her shoulders slumped. As desperate as she was to hold on to the ranch, she wouldn't beg, wouldn't put her childhood friends in an awkward position.

One final chance existed to salvage her situation. She crossed her fingers. "I'm just waiting to hear if I got this grant from the Equine Rehabilitation Fund." With the money from the foundation, she'd be able to bring her mortgage up to date and buy enough feed and hay to see her stock through the winter. Without it, though... She stopped her train of thought. She had to get that grant. She had to.

James's voice dropped to a near whisper. "I've given you six months more than I have any right to, and now I have no choice."

Sarah stared at the floor. She'd exhausted all her other options. The Equine Rehabilitation Fund was her last hope. They'd already had her application for far too long, but any day now, they had to approve her request and send the money she needed. She lifted her head and looked James in the eye. "One month," she pleaded. "That's all I'm asking."

A long minute stretched out while she held her breath and prayed. At last, the bank president held up a finger. "One month, Sarah. That takes us to June first."

Deliberately, she straightened her shoulders. James was going pretty far out on a weak limb to give her this last chance to balance her accounts. She had to make sure he didn't regret it. "I will tell you what," she began. "If I don't have the money by June first, I will walk into your office, I will shake your hand, and I will sign this ranch over to you."

"Well, that's—that's fair." To free up his right hand, James shifted his coffee mug into his left.

Sarah took the hand he extended and gave it a firm shake. "You need me to sign something?"

James lifted the hand she'd just shaken. "You just did."

Sarah hefted her mug. A warmth that had nothing to do with the coffee she swigged spread through her midsection. Despite all her financial woes, returning to Mill Town after graduation had been the right decision. Where else would the president of the bank do business on a handshake?

The reason for his visit concluded, James pointed over her shoulder to the television where the morning talk show had continued. "That guy grew up here," he announced.

Sarah took a second to swallow her coffee. "Bradley Suttons." She nodded. "He used to live next door.

Moved away when he was about thirteen. But I believe he still owns the house."

"I remember." Sympathy tugged at the corners of James's lips. "His parents were killed in that car accident over in Greenbrier."

"Yep." Propping her elbow on the arm she'd folded across her chest, she tipped her coffee cup toward the screen. She'd never known there was such sadness in the world before the day that word of the Suttons' deaths spread through the town. But, as bad as their loss had been for her, it had been so much worse for the boy next door. One minute, her best friend had been a normal kid growing up in a small town with his whole future laid out for him. The next, everything he'd ever known—his parents, his home, his friends— had been stripped away from him.

"He must be about the most famous resident to ever come out of Mill Town." James lifted one eyebrow. "I guess you knew him pretty well?"

"Knew him?" She took a long swallow from her mug. "I was married to him."

Later that evening, she still chuckled at the mix of confusion and surprise that had filled James's face when she'd announced her marriage to Bradley Suttons. Only three people knew of the ceremony that had taken place in her parents' barn that day. She'd never spoken of it. She was pretty sure none of the others had, either. They'd only been thirteen, after all.

And anyway, a mere twenty-four hours later, Bradley's aunt and uncle had whisked him off to Nashville to start his new life.

In the bedroom she'd decorated with hand-me-downs and items she'd found at tag sales, she tugged an old wooden box from beneath the wrought iron bed. Layers of quilts and blankets sank beneath her as she settled onto the mattress and lifted the lid of the treasure box her dad had made. Leather hinges creaked. She drank in the scent of old paper, aged cedar, and memories.

Setting aside the colored pencil drawing that had taken first place in the eighth grade art show, she thumbed through the stacks of ribbons she'd won in riding competitions, the report cards filled with A's, the awards. Her fingertips brushed against velvety softness. There it was, tucked into the corner, right where she'd put it all those years ago. She retrieved the small cloth bag and loosened the drawstring. A diamond solitaire fell into the palm of her hand when she upended the pouch. She held the ring up to the light and smiled, remembering the day she'd wed Bradley Suttons.

When she couldn't find her best friend anywhere in the house crowded with people and hothouse flowers, she'd somehow known he'd be in the old barn. Careful not to ruin her best dress, she'd climbed the rickety ladder into the loft. There, amid the dust motes that danced in the beams of sunlight that seeped through cracks in the barn's wood-slatted walls, she'd found him. He'd been sitting alone, his tightly pressed lips wobbling, his chin tucked down like a bird with a broken wing. She'd plopped down on a bale of hay left over from the previous winter and faced him.

"It's okay to cry, Brad-Bird. I won't tell anyone," she'd promised. Anyone who'd lost his parents was allowed a few tears.

But Bradley hadn't cried. He hadn't even looked up from the shiny surface of his leather shoes. "I can't believe I have to move away from here."

"It'll be fine. You're so smart and everything." She wished she could think of something that would help his heart heal.

"Guess I'm sort of an orphan now. I don't really have a family anymore."

That had to be the worst. The entire Standor family—her grandparents, aunts, uncles and a whole passel of cousins—all lived within walking distance. But Bradley only had one aunt and uncle, and they lived clear across the country in Tennessee. By this time next week, he'd be living with them in a house he'd never seen before, attending classes in a school where he didn't know a soul. She had to do something— anything—to make it better for him, but what?

"Hey." His footsteps heavy, their friend Adam slowly trudged up the stairs to join them. Behind him, loose hay sifted onto the floor below. "I was looking for you guys."

Suddenly, she knew. "Let's get married."

"What?" The look Bradley gave her said she'd lost her mind.

"We should get married." The idea had come to her out of the blue, but it made perfect sense. "Then, we can be each other's family."

Though some of the sadness faded from Bradley's eyes, he shook his head. "We're only thirteen. We can't get married."

"Yes, we can. This is my barn, so I make the rules." She glanced around. From the tack draped across the stair rail to the bales of hay to the sunlight that streamed in through the big sliding door on the ground floor, she knew every inch of the barn as well as she knew the freckles on her arms. She'd raised puppies in the back stall, had taken her first pony ride down the wide middle aisle, felt the velvety noses of her dad's racehorses when she fed them apple slices. The barn was her kingdom, and she dared anyone to tell her what she could or couldn't do in it. Getting married to Bradley was the right thing to do. "You're my best friend, and I say we can do anything we want."

"How are we supposed to get married?" A faint trace of interest crept into Bradley's voice.

"I can marry you." Adam's gaze swung between his two friends. "My dad's a pastor. I've seen him do it, like, a hundred times. It's not that hard."

One look at the hope that gleamed in Bradley's eyes banished all her doubts. Her best friend needed a family. What better way to give him one than for them to get married? Wasn't family what marriage was all about?

Shaking off thoughts from long ago, Sarah slipped the ring onto the fourth finger of her left hand and admired how the light glinted off the diamond. Not that she had any intention of keeping it. She grabbed a sheet of stationary and a pen from the roll-top desk where, among other things, she'd written a dozen letters to the Equine Rehabilitation Fund. Though Bradley's ring had to be worth a sizeable amount, maybe even enough to settle all her debts, it wasn't hers. Not really. The ring belonged to a boy she'd once loved enough to marry. That boy was gone now. He'd grown into a man who'd gotten himself engaged to Catherine Mann. And, without giving herself a chance to reconsider, Sarah began to write.

# Chapter Two

B radley rubbed the petals of the white camellia between his fingers. The blossoms in the vase were real, all right. He shook his head, not understanding the need for such an ostentatious display. He'd whistled when he'd gotten the bill for a bouquet he'd sent Catherine last month, and it had included just one of the fancy blooms. After that, he'd told his assistant to steer clear of the pricey flowers. But Margaret Feldberg, talent agent to the stars, had ordered up a dozen of the expensive blooms, then stuck them in a vase clear across the room where she couldn't even enjoy them. Waste like that was one part of the lifestyle of the rich and famous he didn't think he'd ever get used to. Thank goodness he and Catherine had opted to live a simpler life, starting with their wedding.

Speaking of which…

He'd wandered across to the window while Catherine and her agent discussed upcoming appearances and photo ops. Their conversation had droned on for a while now, but it hooked his attention again when talk drifted to his and Catherine's recently announced engagement. He turned away from the window that overlooked Rodeo Drive.

From her seat in the plush white leather chair behind the ultra-sleek and modern desk, Margaret's voice trilled. "I am getting calls from *People*, from *Vanity Fair*. They all want to photograph your wedding. And they're willing to pay huge!" The middle-aged redhead flung her hands out wide. The tips of her brightly colored nails clawed the air.

"Not gonna happen." Bradley hooked his thumbs into the pockets of his jeans. Though he'd gotten the wind knocked out of him when Catherine had announced their engagement on national television, she'd explained that her enthusiasm had simply gotten the best of her. Now that he'd had time to get used to the idea, he had to admit that having their engagement out in the open had its perks. As long as they were keeping their relationship under wraps, he'd kept his distance from Catherine whenever they were out in public...which was most of the time. With the cat out of the bag, they could act like any engaged couple, and no one would think twice about it.

But he wouldn't allow the paparazzi to turn their solemn exchange of vows into a spectacle. He and Catherine had agreed on a simple ceremony in an Italian vineyard. He dug his thumbs a little deeper into the pockets of his jeans and stood firm. "We want a private wedding."

Catherine shot him a glance filled with promise. "Yes. We want something intimate and personal."

Glad he and his fiancée were on the same page, Bradley barely flinched at Margaret's disbelieving gasp.

"Why?" The agent clutched her chest. With a reverence usually reserved for church, she argued, "A wedding should be shared with those who love you most—your fans."

Bradley stifled a grin. Did Margaret actually think she could change their minds on an issue that was so important to them? While the agent had an uncanny talent for getting her clients' names prominently featured in the press, this was one time when she'd be better off saving her breath, because he and Catherine had made their choice. There'd be no Hollywood hoopla at their wedding.

Though the agent was far too tenacious to give up on the idea, the chagrined expression on Margaret's face told him she'd gotten his message. Pouting, she lifted a thick manila envelope from the corner of the immense slab of polished granite that served as her desk. "By the way," she said, holding out the package, "this came for you."

"What is it?" He sensed a ruse and forced a healthy dose of skepticism into his gaze. Rather than reaching for the envelope that had arrived in the mail pouch his own agent forwarded to Margaret's office each day while he was in L.A., he propped his hands on the back of one of the leather chairs.

"Oh, I have no idea." All breathy innocence,

Margaret dangled the envelope between her fingers. Her breath caught as if a new thought had just occurred to her. "But I bet it's a fan. Writing you a letter for an autograph because they *love* you and they want to be a part of your life." As if she smelled victory, her smile widened. "And that is why you need to share the happy day with them."

Bradley shook his head. *Um, no.* Margaret's act might work on the Hollywood starlets and actors she usually represented, but he knew what he and Catherine wanted. His stomach tightening ever so slightly, he looked to his bride-to-be for confirmation. Relief loosened the knot in his gut when her honeyed laugh sounded through the room. The sparkle in her eyes soothed his fears.

Their united front gave Margaret no choice but to capitulate. "Oh, fine." She tapped the envelope against her fingers. "I'll just give it to the PR department—"

The package dipped at one end. One edge of the padded envelope thunked softly against the desk.

"Wait," Catherine called before Margaret could toss the packet into her Out box. "There's something in there." While Bradley watched, his lovely bride-to-be tore open the envelope. Catherine felt around inside and laughed. "It's from a fan, all right. A fan who's clearly in love with you. She sent you a diamond ring." With a teasing grin, she held it up for them all to see.

When Margaret paired an exasperated sigh with a look that practically accused him of two-timing her client, Bradley took a step back. "I'm sure it's not real," he protested. Though there'd been plenty of opportunities, he'd never, ever so much as thought of another girl since the day he and Catherine had first met.

As if eager to prove him wrong, Catherine studied the ring. "This is a Tiffany-cut one. Half a carat diamond in a white gold setting. And..." She reached into the envelope a second time. "It comes with a love letter."

"Of course it does." Margaret wiggled her fingers in a dismissive gesture.

That ring must've cost the misguided woman a small fortune. Disturbed by Catherine and Margaret's attitude, Bradley stalked to the window. Behind him, paper rustled when Catherine opened the note.

"Dear Brad-Bird..."

*What?* He spun around on a booted heel.

"I saw you on TV." Through pursed lips, Catherine continued reading. "And I couldn't help but remember all those years ago when we were friends. I've thought about you often over the years..."

"Brad-Bird." A smile tugged on his lips as long-forgotten memories of his childhood surfaced. "No one's called me that in ages. Let me see that." He took the note from Catherine and scanned it quickly.

*Sarah Standor.* A rush of emotions rolled over him like a wave at the beach, and his throat tightened.

"First love?" She arched one perfectly groomed eyebrow.

Bradley exhaled a breath that came from somewhere deep inside. "We were thirteen."

"Aw. She was your girlfriend?" Margaret asked, her voice sweet as saccharine and just as real.

"No." Bradley let the paper fall from his fingers onto the table. Hoping she'd understand, he slipped into the chair beside Catherine. "She was my wife."

Every trace of laughter melted from Catherine's face. Her expression both puzzled and demanding, she stared. She wanted an explanation, a good one.

"It was the day of my parents' funeral." Memories of that day swept over him, threatening to drag him back down into those dark times. "I was so sad and lost. I felt alone in the world. Sarah, she, uh—she offered to marry me so I'd have a family." His heart ached with the sweetness of that moment. It was the best gift anyone had ever given him.

Wearing a shy smile, Catherine glanced up from the hands she'd folded neatly in her lap. "That's so nice," she whispered.

"She was a great girl. And this ring." Bradley reached for the diamond his fiancée had discarded on the table like a piece of costume jewelry. "This is my mother's ring."

"I think I'm jealous," Catherine murmured.

Bradley coughed a laugh. If there was one thing in the world the elegant, always perfect Catherine Mann didn't have to worry about, it was another woman. Not where he was concerned. Still, he supposed, even the most beautiful women needed reassurance every once in a while. And that was something he could easily provide. "Nah," he said, rubbing the ring between his fingers, "the girl I remember, she was real skinny, with freckles, and she preferred horses to people."

What had ever happened to Sarah? Or Adam, the friend who'd performed their impromptu—and fortunately for him, illegal—wedding? There'd been a time the three of them had been thick as thieves. Years had passed since he'd last thought of them, or the town where he'd spent the first thirteen years of his life.

He rubbed a hand over his jaw, thinking. "You know, I—I still own my parents' house. I haven't ever been back there since that day." His aunt and uncle had been good people, but they'd never had any children of their own. They hadn't had the first clue about handling one who'd just had everything he'd ever known yanked out from under him. At their urging, he'd shoved all the memories of his childhood home and the life he'd left behind into a mental strongbox and sealed it shut. He hadn't looked inside since. "I should probably deal with that," he admitted, meaning far more than the simple matter of the house.

A new idea occurred to him. There might be an upside to announcing their engagement. Now that they were officially a couple, maybe he and Catherine could go on a little getaway together.

Hoping she'd say yes, he glanced at his bride-to-be. "You know, you should come with me. See where I grew up."

Catherine's features brightened. Leaning forward

until her forehead nearly brushed his, she gushed, "I'd love to."

"Wait! Wait!" Margaret fluttered her fingers in the air. "It's impossible! She's doing a movie." The agent gave an exasperated huff and stared at Catherine. "You're under contract."

Bradley's heart sank, and disappointment tugged at Catherine's lips. From their first date, she'd preached the importance of meeting obligations. Until her movie wrapped up, she had to stay in Hollywood.

As for him, he had all those songs to write for the new album. He should probably stay right where he was and work on them. The best thing to do might be to contact someone in Mill Town, have them handle the sale for him.

"Well." Catherine's hand on his knee told him she had her own ideas about the matter. "Why don't you go back, take care of things, sell the house, have some down time. And, after we get married…" She lingered over a breathy, little smile. "I'll go back with you and see where you grew up." Her voice dropped to a whisper meant for his ears alone. "I'd love to know that part of you."

"I'd like that," he said, meaning every word. He checked his watch and grimaced. He hated to leave, but it was time for him to head for the recording studio. He leaned forward and brushed a kiss on Catherine's cheek. "I'll see you tonight?"

"Mm-hmm." She nodded, though both of them understood that their plans for the evening were tentative at best. Catherine was due on the set in another hour. If today's shoot went well, he'd meet her for a late dinner at one of the trendy hot spots where the importance of being seen by the right people outweighed the quality of the food. And if not, well, there was always tomorrow.

The noise of his boot heels echoed off the walls of the spacious office as Bradley headed for the elevator. His phone buzzed for what had to be the tenth time this hour and, with a resigned scowl, he thumbed through the dozen or so messages that had accumulated. He lingered over the latest one from his assistant. Apparently, this afternoon's recording session had been cancelled in favor of a meet-and-greet with executives from the record company.

Bradley's frown deepened. They probably wanted an update on the delivery of his next album. Which was a problem, considering he hadn't written a single song worth sharing with the band, much less taking into the studio, since he'd come to L.A.

He raked his fingers through his hair. Maybe Catherine's idea for him to go home had more merit than he'd first thought. Getting out of the limelight, escaping the push/pull of people who wanted pieces of him everywhere he turned—it sounded like just the break he needed.

The itchy feeling of anticipation coursed through him, and he flexed his fingers. Going back to Mill Town would be good for him. He'd take care of long-neglected business and put his past behind him, once and for all.

The elevator chimed its arrival. Ignoring it, he took the stairs down to the lobby. The Uber his assistant had arranged to take him to his next appointment waited at the curb behind Catherine's chauffeur-driven town car. Eager, finally, to get back to the business of songwriting, Bradley headed for his ride.

Catherine waited until she heard the elevator doors slide open before she swiveled in her chair to face the woman who sat on the opposite side of the desk. Margaret had been her agent ever since she'd stolen the show in what was supposed to be a bit part when she was six. Over the years, the two of them had grown closer than sisters while both their careers had soared. She knew Margaret had been biting her tongue ever since Bradley had insisted on limiting their wedding to a small, private affair. Now that he was safely out of earshot, she had a pretty good idea of what her agent would say next.

Margaret folded her hands primly in her lap. Her shoulders stiff, she leaned forward. "A small wedding? In Italy?"

"In a way." Fighting the urge to smirk, she nodded. "I've rented an Italian villa and…"

She let the moment draw out as she studied Margaret's approving glance.

"And only invited my *closest* friends." The sprawling

estate would easily accommodate their three hundred guests, plus the caterers, florists, and musicians required for the wedding of someone with their own star on Hollywood Boulevard.

Encouraging Bradley to spend some time in his hometown had been a stroke of sheer genius, if she did say so herself. While he was safely tucked away, she'd be able to finalize plans for their gala celebration without worrying about his reaction. Or his interference.

"I should have known you had a plan," Margaret cooed. "Now, tell me all about it."

A flicker of unease passed through Catherine as she settled in for a nice, long chat with her best friend. She shoved it aside. A wedding was far more than the mere exchange of vows. For people in show business, more publicity was always better. And nothing, not even the Academy Awards, drew more attention than a wedding. In the weeks leading up to the big event, her fans would go crazy! They'd obsess over her gown, her veil, the way she wore her hair. They'd ooh and aah over Bradley's tux, and hearts all over the country would positively melt if he sang one of his love songs during the ceremony. She made a mental note to suggest it.

The man she intended to marry would certainly come around to her way of thinking once he saw what a boost it gave their careers. With that in mind, she brought Margaret up to date on everything she'd done to make her wedding an extravaganza befitting a woman at the top of Hollywood's A-List.

# Chapter Three

*This must be how a goldfish feels.* Bradley eyed the glass walls that stretched to the ceiling above dark, waist-high panels in the president's office of the Mill Town Bank. He propped his Stetson on his knee and leaned back against the dark leather guest chair. He glanced across James Fargo's immense wooden desk and wondered if always being on display had given the man his perpetual squint. Figuring he'd do them both a favor and get the meeting over as soon as possible, he got straight down to business.

"I'm just here for a day or so to sell the house." And, if the muse was kind, start working on a new song for his next album. "I figure there's no point in holding on to it."

James flipped through pages in the folder on his desk. "Well, it looks like you paid off the mortgage years ago. And the, uh, the maintenance staff that takes care of the house is on retainer, so all you need to do is put it on the market."

"Great." The sooner the *For Sale* sign went up,

the sooner he'd head back to Catherine and the life he'd spent the last ten years building. Eager to sign whatever papers were necessary, he glanced at James, but instead of sliding a few forms across the massive desk, the man only stared at the paperwork.

*Uh-oh.* Bradley took in a deep breath and steeled himself against the condolences that were bound to follow.

"I, I, uh, remember what happened to your folks." The bank president gave his wedding ring a nervous twist and swallowed so hard his Adam's apple bobbed. "It, it was a huge shock to this community. One of the toughest things—"

"Sir." Bradley stood. James was obviously ill at ease. So was he, for that matter. He might as well put them both out of their misery. "So, I guess that's all the business we need to take care of."

"Right, right." As if glad to get back on firm footing, James sprang to his feet. "I will put you in touch with Sally Hartford. She's the local real estate broker we use here at the bank. She can put your house on the market, take care of everything."

Bradley bit back a mild oath as, on the other side of the glass wall, a customer hurrying past James's office glanced his way. The woman stopped so suddenly that coffee in the cups she carried sloshed onto the floor while recognition flared in her eyes. Unable, or unwilling, to wrench her gaze off him, she stood in the middle of the corridor wearing the same goofy smile he'd seen on a thousand faces since the night he'd won the Grammy. The familiar expression served as a warning to leave before anyone else noticed his presence.

Turning aside, he extended a hand to James. "I appreciate that, sir. Thank you." He left quickly, his long strides eating up the short distance from the office through the lobby and to the taxi that waited for him at the curb. "Let's go," he told the man behind the wheel seconds before his adoring fan emerged through the bank's doors.

In all likelihood, she only wanted an autograph, maybe a picture of the two of them standing at the entrance to the bank, but experience told him there was no such thing as just one signature, one quick snapshot. Before he knew it, a crowd would gather and it'd be hours before he could break away. As much as he hated to disappoint any fan, he'd been looking forward to enjoying Mill Town's peace and quiet while he settled his parents' estate.

His cell phone buzzed. Hoping Catherine had found a minute to call him—something that rarely happened when she was on set—he pulled the device from his pocket.

Instead of his fiancée's image, a photo of his publicity manager appeared on the screen. Without so much as a single inquiry into Bradley's well-being, the man launched into the most recent list of photo ops, interview requests, and public appearances he'd accepted on his client's behalf.

Bradley shook his head. Earlier in his career,

opportunities like these had been far and few between. Now, so many requests filled his schedule that he had a hard time carving out an hour or two to work on his music. Still, as Catherine often reminded him, if he wanted his songs to stay at the top of the charts, he had to chat with radio show hosts, drop in on late-night television shows, maintain his connection to industry movers and shakers. Suppressing a sigh, he listened while the man on the other end of the line discussed the details of upcoming events.

Sometime later, while the publicist asked about his schedule, he caught a glimpse of lush farmland and a barn from the window of the cab. "Yeah, I'm going to be here in Texas for the next day or so," he answered. "Then, I'm going to head to my studio in Nashville and I'll try to write some more music before I head out on tour."

Through the windshield, he spotted a weathered sign for the Circle M Ranch mounted on rough-hewn logs. When he was a kid, he'd ridden his bicycle past this very spot on his way to school every day.

Resisting the urge to scratch his head, he hurried to end the phone call with a quick, "Hey, I'm going to have to call you back." As soon as he disconnected, he leaned toward the driver. "I didn't give you my address, did I?"

"Aw, everybody knows where your house is." The man behind the wheel turned off the main road onto a familiar dirt track. "You're pretty famous here in Mill

Town. They've got a sandwich named after you down at the diner."

"Really." Bradley chuckled. The driver's Southern drawl was as thick as the cane syrup his mom used to pour over his biscuits.

"Oh, yeah."

Well, what d'you know. A Grammy *and* a sandwich named after him. His star was definitely on the rise. His leather jacket creaking, he pressed closer to the driver. Something about the man's voice triggered a memory of blackboards and white chalk. "I'm sorry, but do I know you?"

"Yeah." The driver stared into the rearview mirror. "We went to school together. Sam Harper."

"Sammy Harper?" Recalling a freckle-faced kid who'd sat beside him in Mrs. Ferguson's music class, he grinned. Sammy and he had been the only boys in the fifth grade who could carry a tune. He relaxed against the seat. "I do remember you."

"Uh, hey. I play lead guitar in a band in town." Sammy glanced over his shoulder. "We play all your hits."

"Great." It was too bad he wouldn't be in Mill Town long enough to stop by and listen, but he'd only be here for a day, two at the most. He pulled a hundred from his pocket while Sammy braked to a stop in front of a two-story house that bore a fresh coat of gray paint.

"Here you go." Bradley handed over the money. He waited just until Sammy tucked the bill into the pocket of a windbreaker before he grabbed his overnight bag and slid toward the door.

"Oh, hey. Don't you want your change?" Sammy asked.

"You keep it." He clapped his childhood friend on the shoulder. Sammy almost certainly needed the money more than he did. The man certainly wasn't going to get rich playing in a cover band down at the local honky-tonk or driving a taxi in a town with a population the size of Mill Town. He should know. He'd worked his fair share of odd jobs and bars before he'd gotten his big break.

For a long moment, he simply stood and watched the dust that rose from behind the departing taxi. This was it. After all these years, he'd finally come back home. What would it be like, walking into the house where he'd spent the first thirteen years of his life? Back then, an icy cold had stung his feet when he'd jumped out of bed before dawn to help his dad milk the cows on winter mornings. By the time they'd finished, his mom had breakfast ready, and the good smells of fried bacon and eggs, biscuits made from scratch and hot coffee had filled the air. Every afternoon, he'd charge down the steps of the school bus and race for the house, eager for a fresh-baked cookie or a slice from one of the pies that cooled on the window over the stove. After supper each evening, their little family would gather in the living room around a crackling fire. While his mom had read aloud from library books, his dad had most often sat in the corner and strummed an old six-string.

He hadn't let himself think of those days in a dozen years or more, and tears stung the corners of his eyes. He took in a deep, cleansing breath and let it out while he won a hard-fought battle over his emotions. Hefting his suitcase, he headed up the sidewalk toward the house that held too many memories of a time he thought he'd forgotten.

Long strides took him past the rose garden his mother had loved. The neatly trimmed bushes fairly bristled with new buds, and that surprised him. He'd half expected to find a thorny thicket of overgrown plants. Someone had obviously been tending the flowers. He made a note to find out who and thank them. As for the rest of the trees and shrubs in the front yard and the climbing vines over the porch, considering the house had been sitting vacant for a more than a decade, he thought they were in pretty good shape.

His footsteps slowed when he reached the back porch. A sudden urge to head straight to Nashville and let the bank handle the sale of the house swept over him.

He shook the thought aside. He'd come here to sort through his parents' belongings, pack up a few mementos of his childhood, maybe write a song or two. The sooner he got started, the better. His purpose renewed, he let a series of firm steps take him up the three stairs to the door, where he dug around in his pocket for the key James had pressed into his hand.

Seldom-used hinges complained when he swung the front door open. He swore he could almost hear his dad playing a mournful tune on the harmonica as he stepped into the narrow hallway that ran the length of the house. His movements stirred the stale, dusty air, and he sighed. Every reminder of the life he'd lived here had been packed away in dozens of boxes that crowded the floor around the bare kitchen counters. In the living room, sheets and heavy plastic draped the lamps, the furniture. More boxes hid beneath a thick coating of dust and dirt.

The rest of the day sped by as he sorted and cleaned and rearranged. Someone had propped his dad's old guitar in the corner. The strings wailed like a troubled cat when he strummed them. He told himself all the instrument needed was a little love—a little tinkering with the fret board, a new set of strings—and it'd be right as rain again, but loss punched him in the gut. He sank onto one of the cloth-covered chairs and mopped his face with one hand.

Even though he knew it was impossible, he'd somehow pictured the house as it used to be, had dreamed of seeing his mom at the stove, of hearing his dad complain about the weather. But those days, and his parents, were long gone. As for himself, he had a new life now, success beyond his wildest dreams, a future to look forward to with a woman he loved and admired.

With that, he took a good, hard look around the room. If he wanted the house to fetch top dollar, no doubt he'd have to do something about the all-around clutter. Shrugging off his jacket, he rolled up his sleeves and set to work.

By the time he had the kitchen squared away, he was ready for a late afternoon pick-me-up. For the first time since his arrival in town, he missed having an assistant on hand to cater to his every whim. As long as he stayed in Mill Town, if he wanted coffee, he'd have to make it himself. But that was okay. He'd done everything for himself during the lean years.

In minutes, he unearthed an ancient coffeemaker from one of the boxes. Two tall shopping bags and a basket of fruit sat on a table in the breakfast nook. Poking through the supplies James had been kind enough to provide, he found everything else he needed. While the rich aroma of a fresh-brewed pot filled the room, he searched for something to pour the coffee into. His gut tightened when he pulled the Best Mom Ever mug from a box of cups and bowls. After tucking it away among the few things he'd take with him when he left, he chose a nondescript mug that had no painful memories attached. Then, figuring he'd accomplished enough for one day, he carried his drink outside.

In the shade of a mammoth oak tree, he sipped the slightly bitter coffee while he rocked back and forth on the glider his dad had erected in front of the house. Mature evergreens dotted the gentle slope down to a graveled road. The view made a good selling point. Or it would, if it weren't for the tumble-down fence that surrounded the ranch next door. A tighter scrutiny of the barns and sheds at the Standors' place revealed loose boards and missing roof shingles on buildings that could use a new coat of paint.

He swigged the last of his coffee. The neighboring ranch had probably changed hands in the years since he'd moved away. Maybe he'd drop by, introduce himself to the new owners and let them know he'd be around for a day or two. He tossed the dregs from his cup on to the grass. There was no time like the present, he told himself as he cut across the field that separated the properties.

Spotting a pick-wielding ranch hand bent over a horse's hoof just inside the gate, he called, "Excuse me, sir. I was looking for the family who used to live in this house." The guy straightened…no, the *woman*, with a decidedly feminine figure.

Despite the warmth that flooded his cheeks, he chuckled. In the years since they'd last seen each other, Sarah Standor had changed. For the better. "There was a skinny little girl with freckles?" he teased.

"I saw an interview you did once where you said you'd come home to Mill Town when pigs fly." Sarah propped her gloved hands on her hips and tipped her head. Her brown eyes sparkled as she stared at the cloudless sky. She lifted cupped hands in the air. "Sky seems clear of swine."

He laughed out loud. That sounded like something he'd say. "Sarah Standor."

"Bradley Suttons." Her wide grin flashed beneath a well-worn cowboy hat. Twin braids the color of burnished copper brushed her shoulders when Sarah shook her head.

"You look…so different." The cocky tomboy had grown into a woman who'd retained all the wholesome good looks of the girl-next-door.

"Well, you seem to have outgrown your awkward phase, too." Her hands regained their purchase on slim hips. "But I don't know if that's true," she corrected herself. "You never had an awkward phase. You're just as handsome as ever. What brings you to town?"

"I'm selling my parents' house." Bradley spared the old homestead a quick glance. "I should have dealt with it years ago, but I never found the time to get back here."

"Well, time does fly when you're busy winning Grammies, becoming a super star." Her smile deepened. "We're all real proud of you."

"Thanks." What else could he say? He shoved his hands in the pockets of his jeans.

"You know, I've been keeping up your mother's flower garden."

"That's real nice of you. She would've appreciated that." Though he was glad to know who to thank for the effort, he couldn't help but wonder why Sarah had spent all that time trimming and caring for the roses. He waited, hoping for an answer while she untied the horse's lead rope from the fence post. When she headed for the barn, he fell in step beside her.

"I felt like it was the least I could do for her. She's the one who taught me how to plant and grow flowers.

Now I have a big garden out back. I supply flowers for most of the local florists."

That seemed like a large undertaking for a ranch like the Standors'. "Your family still raising race horses?" He hadn't been around horses much at all these past few years, but the one that trailed Sarah looked a little soft for Belmont.

"My parents moved to Florida." Sarah's tone drifted up, as if she still couldn't believe they'd moved away. "This place is a horse rescue ranch now. People give me their old horses, their sick horses, and I take care of them." Stepping into the shade of an evergreen tree, she opened the gate to the paddock.

That didn't sound like a lucrative business plan, and probably had something to do with the peeling paint on the side of her house and the fences that needed repair.

Thoughtful, he rubbed a spot on his cheek. It wasn't his place to tell her how to run her ranch. "So you stayed in Mill Town." Ignoring his doubts for the moment, he focused on the woman in front of him. He was enjoying this, the two of them getting to know each other again. It made a nice change of pace to talk to another person without the press or paparazzi or the crazed fans who lately had followed him everywhere he went.

"I stayed in Mill Town," she echoed. "Or rather, I came back to it."

"Why?" Bradley let his gaze follow the road that

led into a town that hadn't changed a bit in all the years he'd been away.

"Why not?" Sarah loosened the rope halter and slipped it over the horse's head.

He could name a dozen good reasons for moving someplace else, starting with the need for a decent cup of coffee. Mill Town certainly wasn't Nashville, where there was practically a Starbucks on every corner. But he guessed Sarah had her own reasons for sticking around. Maybe she'd met someone, started a family of her own. "You married? Have kids?"

"Nope. Not yet." Sarah's mouth drooped into a self-deprecating grimace as she turned the horse out and closed the gate. "I went to veterinary school. And then got busy with the ranch. Guess I just forgot to get married and have children." The sweet music of her laughter filled the air when she tugged on her hat brim.

"Well, Dr. Sarah Standor." He folded his arms across his chest. "I'm glad I had the good sense to marry you when I did."

"That was a no-brainer," Sarah scoffed. Her gaze on a loose fence board, she added, "It was clear I was going to be very successful."

He eyed the slim brunette. Behind that heart-shaped face and those clear brown eyes, Sarah's sharp intelligence gleamed. Add in her work-honed figure, and he bet she could have her pick of the single guys in the county. So why hadn't she married, settled down, found someone who'd shoulder some of the work around here? He shrugged. It really wasn't any of his business.

"You know, Adam's still in town, too."

*Adam?* The kid who'd married him and Sarah had settled down here, too? At his stunned look, Sarah nodded. The news required a comment, and he quipped, "The three musketeers, back together again." Too bad he wasn't going to stick around long enough for a reunion of the old gang. He'd have liked that.

"Um." Sarah hesitated a second before she stared up at him. "How about your fiancée? Is she in town?" Her face colored slightly. "I'm a big fan. I'd love to meet her."

"Nah. She's—she's filming in Los Angeles." A hectic shooting schedule would keep Catherine on the set until the day before their wedding, not that he owed anyone—not even Sarah—an explanation for her absence. "I just wanted to slip into town to handle some business and slip out without any fuss."

Sarah's focus drifted to a spot behind him. "I don't think that's going to happen."

"And why's that?"

"Just, uh…" Sarah's hand on his shoulder turned him to face his childhood home. Cars and trucks littered the hillside like building blocks. Twenty or thirty people milled about on his parents' front yard.

"Whoa!" He instinctively stepped behind the nearest tree. "I didn't know they had paparazzi in Mill Town."

"Oh, they don't." Sarah laughed. "Those are just fans."

Just fans, huh? Prowling about his house as if they owned the place?

Some of his doubt must have shown on his face, because Sarah popped him on the arm. "C'mon. I'll help you." When he remained hidden behind the tree, she beckoned once more. "Come on," she said in a tone that brooked no argument. Without waiting to see if he'd follow, she tossed a question over one shoulder on her way across the yard. "You remember how to ride a horse?"

"Well, it's been a while, but I think so," he admitted as he trotted across the open space between the fence and the barn while the gathering crowd around his house pointed cameras in their direction. "Why?"

Once they stepped inside the darkened barn, where they were out of the sight of his eager fans, Sarah made quick work of saddling two horses. When she handed him a set of reins and told him to mount up, he swallowed, hard. For the last decade, he'd concentrated on getting his career off the ground. There hadn't been time for much of anything else. He hadn't so much as stepped foot on a ranch since he left Mill Town. Then again, he didn't have many options here. He could either spend what was left of the afternoon posing for pictures and signing autographs or ride with Sarah. He opted for the latter.

Leather creaked and dipped when he stuck one foot in the stirrup. Feeling ten kinds of awkward, he tightened his grip on the pommel and hoisted himself aboard. The instant his seat grazed the saddle, the gelding ambled out the barn door behind Sarah and her ride. The hair on the back of his neck prickled as they stepped into the sunlight. From where he sat, the ground looked awfully far away. To add to his misery, his horse obviously had a mind of its own.

"C'mon, now," he coaxed. He put more muscle into his grip on the reins. While Sarah led the way between the barn and a silo, the silly beast she'd given him ignored his firm tug. "No, no," he corrected when the animal balked at following Sarah's lead up a gentle hill. "Over here."

"It's like riding a bicycle," she called. Laughter made her voice shake. "You never forget." She tapped her heels, and her well-behaved mount broke into a ground-eating trot.

Beneath him, his horse's muscles bunched. The next thing he knew, he was holding on for dear life and crying, "Whoa, whoa!" while he bounced in the saddle. But he stuck with it. After all, what choice did he have? He couldn't jump off, not unless he wanted to end up with a broken leg, or worse. He struggled to recall everything he'd ever learned about horseback riding and, by the time they'd gone a half mile, he felt like he just might make it back to the barn without falling off and breaking his neck.

"It's beautiful, isn't it?" Sarah asked as they threaded their way through a copse of trees at the far end of the pasture.

He risked lifting his eyes off a white-knuckled grip on the reins long enough to study his surroundings.

Beneath clear, blue skies, birds chirped from overhead branches. Butterflies flitted among the spring flowers and ferns that grew at the base of mature oaks and maple trees. Sarah was right. The peaceful little clearing held a special appeal. One that felt more than a little familiar.

"Hey, it's our old fort," he said, spying an aging structure in the distance. "You know, I'd forgotten all about this place. Me, you, and Adam built this when we were, like, eleven?"

"Um-hmmm." Sarah reined her horse to a stop beside a shack built of materials they'd scrounged from trash bins and the burn pile. "It's been a doll house. It's been a play house. A girls-only club. A boys-only fort."

When he was a kid, he'd climbed the steps to rescue the fair maiden Sarah with Adam hot on his heels. In his memory, their fortress was a castle, all brick and mortar and moats. Now, he studied the thick layer of pine needles and branches that covered a warped tin roof. Below it, the nails anchoring one of the 2x4s in place had worked loose. The fallen board gave their old fort a crooked smile. Remnants of the curtains they'd fashioned out of old sheets flapped in windows that had never known a pane of glass. He shook his head. "Simpler times."

"Yep." Sarah ran one hand down her horse's neck. "You know, you asked me why I stayed in Mill Town. Well, that's why I stayed. I stayed for the simpler times."

"Right." Good for her. She'd found her niche. He hoped she was as happy with the life she'd chosen as he was with the hustle and bustle that came with living in the spotlight. Not that there was anything wrong with a little peace and quiet, but if he had to exist on a steady diet of it, he might lose his mind.

Each with their own thoughts, they rode in silence for the next hour before Sarah announced that it was probably safe to head back. No matter how much the residents of Mill Town wanted to see their favorite son, she explained, it was nearly supper time, and there were tables to set and meals to prepare. Bradley fought down an urge to argue. In Nashville and L.A., he rarely ate dinner before nine or ten, but Sarah lived here. She knew the habits and customs of the area far better than he did. Sure enough, when he stepped outside the barn after they'd cared for the horses, a single quick glance at his house confirmed that his fans had departed to their own homes and families.

On his way to the gate, he paused. Sarah could have left him to fend for himself this afternoon, but she'd gone out of her way to help him out. He really ought to thank her. "I was thinking maybe we could do lunch. Catch up."

"*Do* lunch?" The laughter that rang through the yard let him know just what she thought about the phrase.

"It's just an expression." Hating the need to defend himself, he shrugged. He might have been born here. Under different circumstances, he might have been content here. But he'd changed. Mill Town was a round hole while he'd shaped his life into a square peg. They no longer fit together.

The petite brunette pinned him with a shrewd, appraising glance. "Well, right now, lunch for me is a sandwich in one hand, and a hammer in the other." She pointed to a sagging rail in a pen that would probably collapse in the next storm. "I've got about a mile of this fence that needs mending."

"Well, you've got fences to mend, and I'm months late delivering a new album." They both had their fair share of troubles, didn't they? "But I think we can spare an hour to catch up. What do you say?"

"Okay." Sarah stopped at an ancient mailbox that stood at the entrance to her ranch. "Meet me here tomorrow. Ten AM. We'll go get Adam. And we will *do* lunch."

"Sounds great." Though ten sounded like an awfully early start, he could handle it. Especially since it meant he'd have the rest of the afternoon to work on the melody that had been playing through his head since he'd stepped into his mom's kitchen earlier today. "See you then."

While Sarah retrieved the day's mail, he headed toward the gate. He'd almost reached it when he heard her call, "Welcome home, Brad-Bird."

He shook his head. "It's not my home anymore." He'd moved on, outgrown both the town and his broken heart. "But thanks."

That evening, after she'd washed, dried, and put away the supper dishes, Sarah carried her coffee mug out onto the back porch. Music drifted down the hill from the Suttons' old place. Leaning against a porch railing, she stopped to listen. Bradley must have found his dad's guitar. He'd been tinkering with it all evening and had finally coaxed a familiar melody from the old box. She joined in as he sang about a man who'd been saved from the depths of despair by a song. Draining the last of her coffee, she smiled to herself. If that wasn't the story of Bradley's life, she didn't know what was.

Tomorrow ought to be interesting. Maybe she should have filled Bradley in on the plans, but it'd be fun to catch him off guard and get him out of his element. She had a feeling, what with the heavy demands of stardom and all, that he didn't have a chance to kick back, be himself very often. It'd be good for him to relax, have a few laughs. Honestly, she could use a little of that herself. In fact, if Bradley had planned to be in town much longer, she wouldn't mind carving an hour here or there from her schedule to spend with him.

And Adam, too. She mustn't forget him. The three of them had sure had some good times when they'd been kids. Now that they were all grown up and all, it might have been nice to hang out together.

She looked toward Bradley's house. It really was a shame that he only planned to stick around for a day or two.

# Chapter Four

B radley braced one hand on the dashboard when
Sarah slammed on the brakes on one of Mill Town's
side streets. The battered old pickup jerked to a stop
in front of a white picket fence, wheels at the curb.
Before he unsnapped his seatbelt, Sarah had already
slid from the driver's seat, slammed the truck's door,
and made it halfway across the street. He hurried to
catch up with her.

"We're late," she called without breaking her stride.

Bradley ran a hand through his hair. What was
going on? Sarah had been prodding him to move
faster ever since his feet had struck her front stoop
this morning. Yeah, sure, he'd been a few minutes late,
but what was the hurry? They were getting an awfully
early start on the lunch rush, weren't they? Or had she
made reservations at some five-star restaurant in the
city?

At that thought, his mouth watered almost
painfully. It had been a while since he'd had to cook
for himself. As a result, dinner last night hadn't been

anything to write a song about. The burger he'd attempted to fry had ended up raw in the middle, charred on the outside, fit only for the trash can. But an upscale restaurant offered possibilities. He could sink his teeth into a nice, juicy steak. Or chicken. As long as someone else prepared it, he could go for chicken. He picked up his pace, hurrying to get close enough to ask where they were headed.

"C'mon." Sarah reached a row of parked cars on the other side of the street and gave him a once-over that reminded him of the way his mom used to examine him before they'd left for Sunday School. "Nice shoes."

"They're Italian." The handcrafted boots probably cost more than her truck.

Clearly unimpressed, she quipped, "They got cowboys in Italy?"

"I wasn't sure what to wear," he confessed. Ever since he'd signed with the recording company, someone else had consulted his schedule and laid out clothing to fit the occasion. Not that he wasn't fully capable of managing his own wardrobe, but Sarah had been strangely close-mouthed about today's final destination.

"Well, you look real good." She trotted up a flight of cement steps to a building that was definitely not the restaurant he'd been hoping for.

"Thanks." At the landing, he tugged open a heavy wooden door and held it for her.

Inside, Bradley fought an urge to scratch his head while he paused to let his eyes adjust to the dim light that filtered through stained-glass windows. White marble glistened from a baptismal font in a nearby alcove. Red carpet led to rows of wooden pews filled with people who listened attentively to the sermon of the day. No wonder Sarah had been in such a tizzy over getting here on time. She should have warned him that she was taking him to church. But what had happened to their plan to meet up with an old friend and have lunch?

"And when we say, do unto others as we would have them do unto us," intoned the minister from behind a wooden pulpit, "we mean more than just follow the commandments. We need to treat others with kindness. And with generosity of spirit."

As he followed Sarah down the aisle, he nodded his apologies to the speaker. His footsteps faltered just as the preacher's voice trailed off.

*Adam?*

From the bemused look on his friend's face, Sarah had managed to pull one over on both of them. Bradley sank down beside her on the pew.

At the front of the room, Adam cleared his throat. "Just ask yourself for one moment," he continued, "how would I like to be treated? What must it be like, to be in that other person's situation?"

Behind Bradley, whispers rippled through the rows of pews. He grimaced and squared his shoulders. From the little he'd heard, it sounded as if his old friend had become a pretty good preacher. He'd hate it if his presence caused a distraction. Resting his back against the hard wooden seat, he decided to set a good example by listening to the sermon. He hoped everyone else would do the same.

Thirty minutes later, he followed the rest of the congregation from the dimly lit church into the bright sunshine. On the concrete landing beyond the heavy doors, he shook Adam's hand.

"Whew!" Adam exclaimed. "I never thought I'd see you back here."

Adam wasn't the only one, Bradley acknowledged with a half smile. He hooked his thumbs over his belt. "I like what you said in there."

"Thanks." Adam gave an amused cough. "But, I should tell you, I got it out of a book, so it's not totally original."

Bradley's smile widened. It was nice to know the ministry hadn't robbed his friend of a sense of humor. "So, lunch?" he asked, refusing to acknowledge the two women who pointed and grinned as they edged past Adam. "You know, I'm really craving sushi."

"Good! 'Cause where we're going"—Sarah and Adam shared a conspiratorial look—"it's about the only thing they got on the menu."

Bradley canted his head. He'd only been in town one day, but he'd already learned to recognize the twinkle that appeared in Sarah's eyes whenever she thought he'd said or done something remarkably dumb. So, where had he gone wrong this time?

The answer to his question came when Sarah braked the old pickup truck to a stop alongside the river instead of in front of an upscale restaurant. Less than an hour later, wearing waders and boots he'd borrowed from Adam, Bradley flipped the bail on the reel Sarah had handed him. Her sassy smile had deepened as she'd informed him that if he wanted sushi for lunch, he'd best get his line wet. As for her and Adam, though, they liked their fish dipped in cornmeal and fried, thank you very much.

He grinned. The sun on his back, the cool water around his knees, the gurgle and ripple of the water passing over the streambed—it all felt like heaven. And even though there hadn't been a single tug at the end of his line, he had to admit he hadn't felt such absolute contentment in a long time. It had been a while since he'd been able to relax around friends who didn't take themselves, or him, too seriously.

"This is real nice." He tossed his line into the current and reeled in as the lure floated back to him.

"You don't remember coming here after church on Sundays when we were kids?" Sarah slowly cranked the handle on her spinning rod.

Bradley ducked his head. "There's a lot about those years I've blocked out." Losing his parents, having everything he'd ever known ripped away from him...it all hurt too much to think about.

"Some wounds just don't heal." On his left, Adam spouted wisdom from beneath a straw hat.

Bradley slipped one finger over the line, prepared

to make another cast. "You know, this feels like Mindful Awareness."

"What?" Sarah's eyes narrowed.

"Ah, it's something Catherine and I do back in L.A." He put some muscle behind the cast this time and congratulated himself when the lure splashed the water near the opposite bank. "We pay to go to this place that does yoga and meditation. They teach you how to be aware of what's in front of you. Let go of the past and the future. Stay quiet. In the moment."

"You're paying money for that?"

When Adam laughed out loud at Sarah's pointed snicker, Bradley looked from one friend to another. Okay, to be honest, the class had been Catherine's idea, but he'd gotten something out of it. At least, he thought he had. "What's so funny?" he demanded.

"You're paying money to sit still and be quiet?" Disbelief raised not one, but both of Sarah's eyebrows.

"You hear that?" Adam scanned the rippling brook.

Bradley tightened his grip on the cork handle of his fishing rod. What was there to hear besides the water rushing past their boots or the occasional cry of a bird on the hunt? "What?"

"That's silence," Sarah pointed out. "It's not yesterday's silence. It's not tomorrow's silence. You're in it right now." She shook her head for emphasis. "And it is free. Of. Charge."

Taking in the blue skies overhead, the soft rustle of the breeze through the trees, the peaceful whisper of the river, Bradley sighed. "I get it." His friends were lucky enough to live in Mill Town, where three cars at the only stop light on Main Street qualified as a rush hour. Of course, they considered a class or two in Mindful Awareness a waste of money. But babbling brooks and quiet moments were far and few between in places like L.A. or Nashville, where so many trucks and cars crowded the roadways that a simple run to the grocery store often involved an hour-long slog through heavy traffic. Determined to enjoy this opportunity as long as it lasted, he reeled in for another cast.

Sarah shot Bradley a side-eyed look as she parked her truck beneath the trees near the barn. He hadn't said a word all the way back from the fishing hole. She guessed she'd been pretty hard on him today: offering him a picnic lunch from her cooler instead of the fancy restaurant he'd probably expected, and then giving him the business about all that yoga and meditation stuff. But that was what friends did. They spoke their minds around one another, didn't they?

She tugged on the edge of her denim jacket. From the little Bradley had opened up about his life, it didn't sound like he had many friends. Oh, he had *people*—acquaintances and fans who toted and fetched for him, who agreed with everything he said. The poor guy probably never knew whether someone actually liked him for himself, or if they just wanted to be around him because he was rich and famous. That had to be tough.

She swept a glance over fences that needed repair, a house that could use a fresh coat of paint, the aged and broken-down horses grazing in the pasture. As desperate as her situation was right now—and she wasn't kidding herself, things couldn't get much worse—she wouldn't trade her life for his.

But at least he had Catherine. He could rely on her to tell him the truth.

She spared Bradley a second look. Though she'd never invade his privacy, she'd love to hear all about her favorite actress. Most weeks, the tabloids featured a picture of the movie star dressed to the nines at one high-brow event or another. She always looked so poised, so confident, both on screen and off. Did Catherine have the same doubts and fears that mere mortals like herself faced?

Would Bradley talk to her about his fiancée? Scrambling out of the truck, she threw caution to the wind.

"So, tell me about Catherine," she said, lifting the cooler from the truck bed.

Bradley came around from the passenger side, his hands tucked inside the pockets of his jeans. "She's beautiful. Smart. And she's very talented."

"Well, I know that much from reading *People Magazine* at the dentist's." She prodded his shoulder. "C'mon. What's she really like?"

"Well, she's funny. She's got a huge heart."

She listened closely as Bradley talked about the generous donations Catherine made to worthy causes each year. The idea that someone with all that ethereal beauty was also kind and giving warmed her from the inside out.

"She's been famous since she was a kid, so, she's used to it. You know?" His booted feet stirred up tiny dust clouds as they walked toward her front gate. "She taught me a lot."

"You are a lucky guy." It sounded like Bradley had found the perfect woman for himself.

"I know." His face colored slightly. "No one for you?"

Well, she should have expected him to ask about her love life. Turnabout was fair play among friends, after all. She tipped her head back. "Oh, there was someone once, but not anymore."

"Why?"

"Well, we wanted different things. I wanted a real commitment, and he wanted..." She laughed to cover the dull ache that still bothered her whenever she thought of the relationship that had died a messy death in the middle of her senior year at veterinary school. "The opposite?" Her heart had flat-out broken when she'd discovered that the man she'd pinned all her hopes on had still been playing the field.

"Sorry." The murmured apology sounded as if it came straight from Bradley's heart.

She brushed a strand of hair from her face. "Yeah, well. It didn't matter. He wasn't the one."

She supposed she should try again to find her real Mr. Right. The one who'd never cheat or lie.

But between caring for the horses and the dogs, and keeping up with the other chores that came with running what amounted to a shelter for abused and discarded animals, dating didn't even have a spot on her To-Do List. Besides, she had bigger issues than finding a boyfriend or going on a date.

She lifted the door to the mailbox and took a hopeful peek inside. A tiny spider busily spun a web in one corner. Otherwise, the box was as empty as it had been when she'd checked it yesterday.

Disappointment sent a cold shiver through her. What was taking the Equine Fund so long? Nearly two weeks had passed since she'd given her word to James Fargo. In two more, she'd lose the ranch, her horses, everything. She let the lid slam shut and stalked past Bradley.

"What's wrong?" Concern roughened the voice adored by millions.

"I'm just..." Setting the ice chest on the ground, she slid her hands into her back pockets. When they were just kids playing in the old fort, Bradley had always wanted to be the knight in shining armor who rescued the princess in distress. She hadn't known this grownup version of her childhood friend long, but she sensed he had a good heart. If Bradley ever found out about her financial woes, would he insist on helping her out? She hoped not. She had her pride, and the last thing in the world she wanted was to take advantage of their rekindled friendship. Besides, the Foundation was bound to fill her request soon. When it did, she'd have enough to pay off her mortgage, bring her bills up to date, and save the ranch. "I'm waitin' on a letter that hasn't arrived yet."

The moment stretched out. She crossed her fingers and hoped he wouldn't ask any more questions. Relief shuddered through her when Bradley finally sighed.

"Well." He scuffed one boot on the walkway that led to her front door. "Thanks again for everything. It was really great to see you and Adam." He took a breath. "I'll probably leave town soon, so I'm glad we got to catch up."

"Yeah." She exhaled the breath she'd been holding. It had been nice. Nicer than she'd expected, considering how famous he was and all.

"And thanks for sending that ring."

She grinned up at him. "I'm happy you're finally going to use it on a *real* bride."

When Bradley's laughter hit a false note, she gave herself a mental kick in the pants. He'd probably given Catherine one of those huge, sparkling diamonds that had cost as much as her house. It was just as well he was heading back to Nashville soon. The citizens of Mill Town were just simple, ordinary folks. They didn't much go in for all that flash, or people, like Bradley, who needed it. She leaned in for a neighborly hug. "It was great to see you, Brad-Bird."

"You, too."

"Take care." She hefted the cooler and headed for the house, a little sad that their time together had ended but thankful they'd had a chance to reconnect.

Sitting on the front porch of his parents' house that evening, Bradley ripped a sheet from the yellow legal pad, crumpled it into a ball, and sent it flying. Why wouldn't the words come to him? With no concerts to perform, no appointments to keep, no fans begging for autographs and pictures, staying in Mill Town gave him the perfect opportunity to work on a song for the new album. Yet, he still couldn't put two lines on the paper without crossing them out and starting over.

He tapped his pencil against the wicker table. The reps from the record company had been hounding him for something upbeat and peppy, a departure from the ballads he usually sang. The change, they said, would breathe new life into his music. That was all well and good for them, but he'd been racking his brain all afternoon and hadn't come up with a single line, much less an entire song.

Across the valley, a train whistle blew. Long and low, the melancholy note broke the silence of the quiet night. In the distance, crickets chirped. A warm breeze riffled the pages of his notepad. An owl hooted from a perch on a nearby tree branch. The sounds brought back memories of simpler days, simpler ways.

Humming the tune that had been playing in his head ever since he'd walked into the kitchen yesterday morning, he leaned over the guitar that rested on his knees. Almost by itself, his pencil moved across the page, jotting down the story-song of a cowboy faced with the decision to stay where he was or pack up and move on.

Bradley grabbed a guitar pick and ran through the music, stopping at the end of one line to correct a word, at the end of another to find a rhyme. The chorus was tricky. He lingered over it, trying out different phrases until he found the right ones. After playing through it a few times, he glanced down at the sheet of paper. The song wasn't perfect—not yet—and it certainly didn't have the hard-rocking beat his rep expected. But it had potential. Real potential. Better yet, his mouth wrapped around the words naturally, unforced. Over the next few days, he'd tweak a word here, a phrase there, smooth out the rough spots and polish the transitions. When he finished with it, his fans would love it. He could feel it in his bones.

He leaned back against the wicker sofa. Down the hill, the light in Sarah's kitchen winked out. She'd probably turned in. He should, too, and he would… in a little while. For now, he was perfectly content to sit right where he was and let the night sounds drift over him.

# Chapter Five

Sunlight played across Bradley's closed eyelids. The sweet scent of flowers wafted in the warm spring air. Waking, he stretched and looked around to get his bearings. *Well, I'll be.* He'd fallen asleep on the wicker sofa, one arm tucked under his head, his feet dangling off the end.

He hadn't slept outside in… He thought back to the nights when Adam, Sarah, and he had been best buds. The three of them had spent many a night roasting hot dogs over a campfire near the old fort and feasting on s'mores. When their bellies were so full they couldn't possibly eat another bite, they'd lain on their backs and searched the sky for shooting stars. Those had been the days.

Hauling himself upright, he rubbed the sleep out of his eyes. Dew had dampened the yellow legal pad he'd been working on the night before, but the ink was still legible. He reached for it. He ran through the set of lyrics, more than a little surprised that they sounded just as good to him in the light of day as they had in the dead of night. Even better, the ghost of another song had come to him in his dreams. Or maybe in his memories of days past.

Excitement thrummed his chest. Wherever the song had come from, the log jam that had stymied him these past few months had finally broken. Flipping to a dry page, he jotted down a couple of quick notes. Reluctant to leave the porch now that his creative juices had finally started flowing again, but desperate for a cup of coffee and a bathroom, he tucked the pad under one arm, stuck the pencil behind his ear, and headed inside.

At the table in the breakfast nook a short while later, he sipped a much-improved version of the bitter brew he'd made the day before. He added a little bit of sugar and patted himself on the back. Give him another day or two, and he'd get the hang of this coffee pot. He picked at the threads of the second song while he drank his first cup. Relief swept through him when the melody didn't unravel and the words to match it started coming together. Eager to see where the muse would lead this time, he tinkered with the first verse.

He worked for an hour, and then the words stopped flowing. He shrugged. Sometimes that happened. In the past, he'd often crumpled the paper into a ball and pitched it into the trash. But somehow, that reaction didn't feel right this time. With silence pressing in all around him and nothing else demanding his time, he opted for a change of pace instead and unpacked a few boxes in the living room. While he worked, the song percolated inside him. Whenever a new line gelled, he stopped what he was doing and scratched the words out on the legal pad he kept nearby.

The day passed as he alternated between writing and getting the house in order. He kept at it after supper and worked till the moon rose against a star-filled backdrop. By the time his eyes felt gritty and his fingers cramped around the pencil, he had the bones of at least three new songs, maybe more. He carefully set the pages aside and called it a night then, certain he'd pick things up where he left off in the morning.

Fatigue and exhilaration swirled within him as he trudged up the stairs to the attic, where his mom had stored extra bedding in a sturdy chest. The tangy smell of cedar filled his nose when he opened the lid. Even after all these years, the fragrant wood had protected the pillows and blankets. He scooped them into his arms and eyed the teddy bear that lay at the bottom of the chest. A chuckle escaped his lips. He'd loved that old bear so much he'd rubbed holes in the animal's patchy fur. Grabbing it, he frowned at the stuffing that poked out from several spots. The poor thing should have been relegated to the trash bin long ago. He dropped the tattered toy back into the trunk and closed the lid. But he made it only as far as the stairs before an urge to hang onto his childhood treasure forced him to retrace his steps. Moments later, he carried the bear downstairs with him. If nothing else, it had earned a place on a shelf. One day, maybe he'd show it to his own kids, if he and Catherine were lucky enough to have them. Who knew? He might even write a song about an old bear who spent years wishing for a much-loved owner to return home to rescue him.

Before he turned in, he gravitated to the porch where he put his heart and soul into belting out the words to the cowboy song. When he reached the final chorus and strummed the final chord, the echo of the tune reverberated in the still air, and he smiled.

Today had been a good day. He hadn't been this productive in ages. For as far back as he could remember, he'd dreaded the time when he'd have to return to Mill Town. But he'd discovered that he'd had nothing to fear and, as long as his creative juices were flowing, he probably ought to take advantage of the break. He nodded to himself. He'd stay put for a few more days, write some more songs, and get the house ready to put on the market. The decision made, he headed inside, where he fell into a sound sleep between sheets that smelled of cedar and home.

Muffled voices woke him out of a sound sleep. The door to the bedroom burst open.

"Not many of these older houses have two ovens." In a voice that practically gushed with a fervent passion, a slim woman wearing office attire steered a casually dressed couple toward the closet. "And *three* bedrooms."

"Hey! What's going on?" Grabbing the covers, Bradley bolted to a sitting position. He gave the strangers who'd just barged into his room a bleary-eyed glare.

"Oh!" The woman in the suit loosed a startled gasp. She clutched a clipboard to her chest. "You're still here! I'm sorry. I thought you left days ago."

"Well, I didn't," Bradley grumbled. Someone had clearly gotten their wires crossed. He'd only been in town a couple of days. He reached to rub the sleep from his eyes and realized he'd been holding onto his old teddy bear.

The bear flopped onto the quilt. *Oh, geez.* Superstars didn't sleep with stuffed animals. He grabbed the memento from his childhood and stuffed it under the sheet.

Was there a chance his early morning visitors hadn't recognized him? *Nope.* The woman in jeans gawked at him like a love-struck teenager while she pawed through her purse, no doubt searching for her phone to take pictures.

"I'm Sally Hartford, the real estate broker." Ms. Hartford's hand found purchase at the waist of her suit skirt. A wobbly smile widened her lips. "Mr., uh, Fargo from the bank sent me."

Bradley fought an urge to slap his head. No one knew his plans had changed. "I decided to stay awhile."

The client at Ms. Hartford's side aimed her phone. Bradley barely had time to throw his hand up in front of his face before she snapped the first picture. Speaking so fast she stumbled over the words, she prattled, "Would you mind if we took a little...? It would mean so much. Hon, you take it." She shoved her purse and assorted items at the bespectacled man beside her and, without waiting for an invitation, plopped down on the mattress.

Bradley cringed when the springs squeaked. Could this moment get any more embarrassing? The tabloids would pay a king's ransom for pictures of him in bed with some strange woman. As for Catherine... Heat burned his cheeks.

"Maybe..." Ms. Hartford's tone doused a bucket of cold water all over her client's enthusiasm. "Maybe we should let Mr. Suttons wake up a bit and, uh—"

"That'd be nice," Bradley agreed quickly.

"—and, uh, put some clothes on," she ended in a whisper.

"I don't mind." Though disappointment clouded the woman's features, she rose slowly.

"We'll come back later." Ms. Hartford threw the comment over her shoulder while she practically shoved both her clients from the room. *Sorry*, the real estate agent mouthed as she closed the door firmly behind her.

Bradley expelled a breath.

The air had barely crossed his lips before the door popped open again. Ms. Hartford's face reappeared in the opening. "I love your music. You're my favorite singer. You probably don't remember me, but we went to school together? I used to be Sally Brunswick?" She laughed as if uncertain of her name, the time of day, or even where she was.

"Yeah, no. I—I'm sorry. I don't." For Pete's sake, he hadn't even had a cup of coffee yet. His brain wasn't firing on all six cylinders.

"Okay." The fact that she'd been trying to carry on a conversation with a groggy, half-dressed superstar must have finally sunk in. Sally's voice dropped to a whisper. "I'm just going to go now." This time, when she closed it, the door stayed shut.

Bradley shook his head and laughed. What else was there to do? He'd told Jimmy Fargo he wanted to sell the house as soon as possible, but he hadn't bothered to tell anyone that he'd changed his mind about staying on for a few days. So, he supposed he was at least partly to blame for this morning's surprise visit. Well, at least no incriminating pictures had been snapped, no videos taken. If it happened again, though, he might not be so lucky. To make sure there wasn't a next time, he'd swing by Sarah's and tell her he'd be sticking around for a few days…as soon as he put on some decent clothes.

Sarah snipped the stem of a perfect blue iris and immediately plunged the cut end into a bucket of fresh water. "That's fifty-five and the last of them," she murmured. The florist had requested four dozen of the elegant flowers for the Thompson wedding, but she always provided a few extras. And she wasn't alone. The women of the Ladies Auxiliary usually baked two cakes, not one, for the annual Cake Walk. At the ice cream parlor, the sales girls added an extra scoop to each cone. Going above and beyond the need of friends and customers was just part of Mill Town life, part of what made living here so special.

Tucking the snippers into the back pocket of her jeans, Sarah rose. Her knees protested the hours she'd spent in the flower garden this morning, but the job was worth the effort. The money she'd make on this delivery would cover her bill at the feed store for another week.

She stretched and rubbed her back where the muscles had knotted while she'd bent over the plants. A smile tugged at her lips. Beneath the shade of towering maples, healthy blooms and waxy leaves swayed in the light breeze. A heady scent of roses mingled with the sweetness of the peonies. Marigolds and carnations added a sharper note, and she inhaled a lungful of the heavenly smell before she hefted the heavy bucket and tucked it in among the rest of her orders in the back of her truck.

"Best get these delivered," she told the dogs that waited for her at the garden gate. "Ya'll mind the ranch while I'm gone, and there'll be a treat in it for you when I get back."

Driving slowly so as not to jostle the cut flowers any more than necessary, she followed the graveled track that led toward the main road. As she passed by the Suttons' place, she spotted Bradley bent over his daddy's old guitar on the swing out front. She gave him a passing wave, but her plan to mosey on into town changed when he motioned her to a stop.

"Hey!" He shoved the guitar aside and hustled down the hill toward her. "Those are beautiful."

"Thank you." She shifted into Park, but left the motor idling. "I'm just driving them into town to some of the florists. We got three weddings this weekend." The designers would stay busy all week turning the blossoms into table arrangements and wreaths and such. "I really think it's the flowers that make a wedding."

"Yeah." Bradley's head bobbed just enough to tell her he didn't have much of an opinion on the subject.

Poor guy. He was probably feeling a little lonely. After he'd stopped by to tell her he was sticking around a little while longer to work on his music, she'd put the word out that everyone needed to respect his privacy. As far as she knew, he'd been holed up in the house for the past two days, just him and his guitar. Did he need a break?

"You know what?" she asked, making a spur-of-the-moment decision. "Tomorrow morning, I'm gonna *do fishing*, if you want to come."

Bradley laughed out loud. "You're going to *do fishing*, huh?"

His reaction warmed a spot in her heart, but she pursed her lips and put her best efforts into mimicking the serious scowl he sometimes wore. "That's just an expression."

"Is it now?" Bradley's raised eyebrows told her he was onto her joke.

The laughter she'd been trying so hard to suppress escaped to join his. When she stopped giggling, she asked, "You want to come?" She doubted he would. She and Adam had tricked him into going with them on Sunday, but surely, a country music superstar had better things to do than wet a line at the old fishing hole.

Apparently not.

At Bradley's quick, "Yeah, sure," she put the truck in gear. She had flowers to deliver and, now that she had a fishing partner, she'd make a stop at the grocery store to replenish her supply of lunch meat and sodas. After all, someone like Bradley would expect more than her usual PB&J with a side of water.

On her trek to the barn, Sarah caught a snatch or two of Bradley's voice along with the faint strum-strum of his guitar. She snugged her vest a little closer and smiled. As long as Bradley was working on his music, she could take her time with the horses this morning. Which was a good thing because, despite a calendar that said they were well into spring, temperatures had taken a nose dive the night before. The horses burned more calories trying to stay warm on days like this, and it'd take longer than usual to dish out the extra rations of hay and oats they needed.

Two hours later, as she loaded the rods and reels, the ice chest, and a couple of folding chairs into the back of her pickup, Sarah crossed her fingers.

Daybreak offered the best odds of catching a fish, and they were getting a late start. Still, she hoped Bradley would get his first bite today. She'd love to show him how to set the hook, to coach him through the art of landing a big one. She couldn't wait to see his reaction when he held a wriggling, glistening fish in his hands. It sounded like his life in the big city kept him far too busy to enjoy the simple pleasures of standing in a stream of icy-cold water while the sun warmed his back and a trout tugged at the end of his hook.

A short time later, she stared down at a mass of knotted line on her spool and bit back an urge to laugh. Here she was, supposedly showing the town's guest of honor the ropes, and she'd netted a terrific backlash with her first cast. Meanwhile, the man beside her tossed his line into the fast-moving current as if he'd been doing it all his life. Gritting her teeth, she set to work untangling the mess.

"You know, I haven't felt this relaxed in a long time." If he noticed he was the only one fishing, Bradley was kind enough not to mention it. "I'm usually running to catch a plane. Or play in a concert."

"Well, that sounds excitin'." She freed just enough line to set the bail. With her next cast, the lure plunked into the water not five feet from where she stood. *Great.* At this rate, she'd go home empty-handed and there'd be no supper on the table tonight.

"It was. At first. But it gets old fast. Waking up in a different hotel suite every morning. Not knowing what city you're in until you open up the door and look at the newspaper. *The Cincinnati Post. The Oregonian. The New York Times. L.A. Times.*"

She and Bradley definitely operated on different planes. Why, he was so busy complaining about life at the top of the heap, he hadn't even noticed that she'd barely gotten her lure wet. She gave him a sidelong glance. Bradley was a nice guy. He probably had no idea how he sounded to someone who'd never lived among the rich and famous. Maybe all he needed was a gentle reminder that many people would kill to live the life he led. But who would tell him? He didn't seem to have a lot of friends. At least, not the kind who'd clear their schedules and come to Mill Town with him. That left just her. Sucking air in over her teeth, she gave him her best smirk.

"Yep. All those first-class flights. And fancy hotel suites. And big bank accounts. Being rich and famous sounds rough."

"You're making fun of me again." Bradley inclined his head.

"Am I?" She hiked her eyebrows. "I thought we were just catching up."

Although, so far, Bradley had been the only one doing the talking. How would he react if she confessed her fears, her problems?

She shook her head. Someone like Bradley probably couldn't understand what it felt like to mark off the days on the calendar, knowing that every day that passed brought her one day closer to losing everything.

# Chapter Six

"Yeah, I don't know what it is about being back here in the house I grew up in, but I'm writing music like I did years ago. I mean, it's just flowing out of me."

"That's great. I'm so happy for you." Standing on the raised platform before the three-way mirror in L.A.'s most exclusive bridal salon, Catherine watched the sales consultant fluff the delicate chiffon on a gown that, even by her standards, cost a pretty penny. Was it worth the price? She struck a kittenish pose. The layers of gossamer fabric rippled.

Oh, yes! This was *it*. This was the gown. She had to have it, no matter what the cost. With a wave of one finger, she signaled Margaret to cue the rest of the bridal party.

"I'm not going to Nashville," Bradley's voice sounded in her ear. "I'm gonna stay here and write."

*Good.* The longer he stayed tucked away in some little-bitty town where there was absolutely no chance of him running into one of the horde of journalists and reporters who'd be covering their wedding, the more she could focus on finalizing her plans. Though, to tell the truth, if she'd had any idea how much work throwing the party of the decade involved, she might have opted for something a tad simpler. Not the Plain Jane affair Bradley had in mind, of course. Why, if she didn't at least hire a string quartet to play the wedding march, her friends would all assume she was washed up, a has-been. No, what she had in mind would definitely leave everyone with the right impression: that she and Bradley were at the top of their game... and still climbing.

Besides, they weren't a pair of lovebirds like the ones in her last movie. Theirs wasn't some sappy, sentimental union. No, what they had was more of a business relationship. Oh, sure, she definitely liked Bradley. She even loved him...in her own way. She'd be a fool not to, and she was no one's fool. Bradley truly was a sweetheart. He treated her better than anyone she'd ever dated.

But once they returned from their honeymoon, she'd go straight to work on her next big picture while her brand-new husband crisscrossed the country on his record tour. As for their future, things would go on pretty much as they had been. With her career centered in Los Angeles and his in Nashville, she didn't see the point of trying to set up house together. It wasn't like she planned to quit acting and become a housewife or anything. At that ridiculous thought, her smile tightened.

Suddenly aware that the man on the other end of the phone had stopped talking, she filled the gap with the words she knew he wanted to hear. "I miss you."

"Yeah, uh, you know, I—I wish you were here. I could take you out on a long hike before dawn and then fishing in the creek."

"That sounds *lovely.*" Catherine paused to give herself a pat on the back. No one in Hollywood could have poured more sincerity into a line that was so patently false. She pulled her cell phone away from her ear for a second. Did Bradley honestly think she was the kind of girl to go hiking and, ugh, fishing? He couldn't be serious. She got plenty of exercise... in a perfectly air-conditioned gym. As for the other, watching her stunt double wade into a fake stream on the movie set last year was as close as she ever intended to come to a fishing rod or those slimy things that dangled from hooks.

She glanced up to watch a parade of young starlets hand-picked for their symmetry and grace form a line of perfectly matched attendants. As glad as she was that things were going well for Bradley—and she was, really she was—it was time to dial back his enthusiasm for all things country. "I'm so excited to see you in Italy for our wedding." She shot Margaret a questioning glance.

From her perch on the arm of a plush leather sofa, her agent signaled the attendants. "Now, turn."

On cue, the actresses spun in lazy circles. Catherine caught her breath. In the icy blue gowns with their crystal-studded halter tops, her attendants looked like Greek goddesses. Second tier, to be sure, but their near-beauty complemented her stardom. *Perfect.*

"Now, just you and me and the Italian countryside, right?"

*And about three hundred of our friends and business associates.* As well as a hundred or so caterers, florists, and wait staff who would see to their guests' every need. Plus, reporters from every major media outlet.

Still holding onto her cell phone, Catherine managed to cross her fingers. "Of course. I mean, there are some minor details to consider. It isn't a wedding without flowers and a cake. I've been so busy working, I've hired someone to take care of all that."

That was her out, her excuse. If Bradley objected to any part of the extravagant plans she'd made, she'd just blame it on the wedding planner. She grinned as two adorable little girls decked out in silky skirts and matching headbands joined the rest of the bridal party. The children hit their marks like the pros they were. Choosing child actresses to act as flower girls had been a stroke of genius. She'd have to remember to thank Margaret for suggesting them.

Bradley's voice rumbled in her ear. "Well, I just want to get married in a place that reminds us that being together is all that matters. Some place where the world can't find us."

Aw, he always said the perfect thing. She supposed that was one of the reasons she was marrying him. His old-fashioned notions about weddings aside, they were perfectly suited to each other. "Just you and me where the world can't find us. That sounds wonderful." And they'd have it…after the wedding. She'd make sure they spent two whole days of their honeymoon alone, not a single reporter in sight.

"Good," Bradley said. "I'll see you soon."

"Another turn." Margaret aimed her camera.

Catherine propped one hand on a cocked hip while her bridal party slowly rotated. Yes, she nodded. Everything was exactly the way it was supposed to be. Bradley might think he wanted a quiet ceremony in the middle of a vineyard where no one could find them, but once images of their picture-perfect wedding were splashed across the front pages of every tabloid from New York to L.A., he'd thank her for the boost she'd given both their careers.

Bradley flexed his fingers to work out the kinks that came from his latest three-hour songwriting session. He'd meant it when he'd told Catherine the music was flowing. After months of not being able to draft so much as a shopping list, he couldn't believe how good it felt to put pen to paper and actually write song after song. Why, if he stuck around here another week or so, when he did get to Nashville, he'd probably be able to go straight into the recording studio and come out with a complete album.

His stomach rumbled a reminder that he hadn't eaten anything since breakfast. He anchored his notes down beneath a paperweight he'd unearthed from one of the boxes in the living room. That done, he fixed himself a sandwich, which he ate over the sink while he enjoyed the view out the kitchen window. Feeling the need to stretch his legs a bit and maybe share a little company before his next writing session, he wandered down the hill to the Standor ranch.

In the main yard, he looked around for Sarah. She was nowhere to be found, so he ambled toward the barn. There, the smell of leather in the tack room mingled with the earthy scent of horses and hay, just as it had done when he was a kid.

How many times had he climbed to the top level with Adam in hot pursuit, both of them determined to rescue Sarah from the evil villain of the day? How many lazy afternoons had they escaped the summer heat by plopping down on top of a hay bale with their library books? Or swung from the rope in the loft? Too many to count, that was for sure.

Those carefree days had come to an abrupt end the day his parents had died. Before the week was out, his aunt and uncle had whisked him off to Nashville, where he'd begun a new chapter in his life. There, in a bedroom that had held no reminders of his past, in a neighborhood where all the houses had looked alike, he'd found comfort in his music. In the end, the move had served him well, but he often wondered how his life would have turned out if he'd stayed in Mill Town, if he'd never left, if the accident had never happened.

Awash in memories of the day his life had taken a

hard left turn, he mounted the stairs into the loft. He studied the spot where Adam had married him and Sarah. They'd come here straight from the funeral, so the three of them had already been wearing their Sunday best. Sarah had sworn they couldn't have a wedding without flowers and had pinned boutonnieres to his and Adam's suit coats. He'd never asked her where she'd gotten either them or the bouquet she'd carried but, looking back, she must have plucked the flowers from a couple of the funeral arrangements. Goodness knew, there'd been enough of them. He was pretty sure, between the wreaths and baskets at the gravesite and the ones that had filled the house, there hadn't been a single blossom left in all of Mill Town. Adam had insisted he had to have a Bible to make things official, but none of them had wanted to risk sneaking back into the house where well-meaning relatives might ask what they were up to. Without a copy of the Good Book handy, the preacher's son had grabbed the first one he'd been able to lay his hands on—Sarah's history textbook—and they'd gathered in front of hay bales they'd lined up like pews.

"And because you're best friends, and because you want to be family forever, I ask you, Bradley, will you take Sarah to be your wedded wife forever?" A shaft of afternoon sun glinted off Adam's braces. "Do you promise to care for her? And obey her?"

"Wait. Obey?" He wasn't at all sure about that. Sarah could be a bit on the bossy side. "That's in there?"

Adam shrugged. "I think so."

He glanced at Sarah. Her eyes reflected his own nervousness. Somehow, that eased his fears. "I guess I do."

"And I promise, too." Sarah snugged the bouquet of flowers a little tighter to her chest.

Adam glanced down at the script he'd tucked between the pages of the text book. "Oh, do you have a ring?"

A tiny flicker of panic eased when his fingers touched the small velvet sack he'd borrowed from his mom's jewelry box. He loosened the drawstring, pulled out the silver circle topped by a sparkling stone.

"It's really pretty." Sarah sounded surprised, as if she'd expected nothing more than a plastic toy from the Cracker Jack box.

"It's my mom's."

The atmosphere in the old barn changed the moment he spoke the words. Became more serious, more real. He wasn't the only one who felt the change. Sarah's eyes grew so wide, he almost thought they'd pop out of her head.

"Now, repeat after me." Adam swallowed. "With this ring…"

"With this ring," he repeated.

"I thee wed."

"I thee wed." Taking Sarah's hand, he slipped the slender band onto her finger.

For a long moment, none of them moved. He wasn't sure about the others, but he didn't think he'd even breathed.

"Oh!" Adam's exclamation broke the spell. "I now pronounce you married. You may kiss the bride."

He froze then, uncertain what to do next. He'd never kissed a girl before, and he wasn't about to start with Sarah. Especially not with Adam standing there, staring at him.

Lucky for both of them, Sarah solved the problem. As if daring him to try anything, she balled her fist and punched him on the arm. He followed her lead—back in those days, he usually did—and did the same.

A short while later, the friends and relatives who'd gathered after the funeral began trickling out of the house. His aunt called him inside. When he left for Nashville the next day, he felt a little less alone knowing he'd always have Sarah's friendship to fall back on.

"Memories?"

Startled from the flashback, he turned. He'd been so lost in that long-ago day that he hadn't even heard Sarah climb the steps. Dressed in jeans and a long-sleeved T-shirt, she stood at the top of the stairs. "Yeah," he admitted.

"Well, it hasn't changed much, has it?" She strode across the hay-strewn floor toward him.

"Not a bit."

"So how's your songwriting going?" As if she didn't know what to do with them, she tucked her hands in the back pockets of her jeans.

"Great!" The stock answer rolled off his tongue, but for the first time in months, he meant it.

"Good."

When Sarah expelled a breath he could only describe as relieved, he congratulated himself. Re-establishing their friendship had been an unexpected bonus of the trip back home. He felt he could tell her just about anything and, squaring his shoulders, he prepared to do just that.

"I just made a decision. This is where I want to get married." Everything about that long-ago day when he and Sarah had stood before Adam brought back feelings of warmth, of being loved. He wanted to relive that moment. To recreate it for him and Catherine.

Sarah's eyes stretched open until they were nearly as wide as they'd been on the day they'd swapped vows in this very place. "You can't get married here."

"Why?" Bradley frowned. Once he moved a few hay bales out of the way and swept the dirt and straw from the floors, there'd be plenty of room. Chickens clucking from their nests and the gentle neighs of the horses would add a little real-world ambiance to the special day.

"Uhhhh." Sarah's mocking laughter told him she thought the reasons should be obvious. They weren't. At least, not to him. Searching for an explanation, he scoured her face and waited. "Well, it was fine for a pretend wedding when we were kids, but Catherine Mann will not want to get married here." Sarah's whole body shimmied when she shook her head.

"You don't know her like I do," he pointed out. Born into Hollywood royalty, Catherine had grown up surrounded by wealth and the privileges of the very rich. At first, he'd thought she loved the life she led, but he'd been surprised to learn over dinner one night that she longed to escape the glitz and glamour as much as he did. Though they hadn't made any concrete plans, he knew what he wanted, what they both wanted. "She wants to live a normal life, but she just doesn't know how."

He wasn't fooling himself. He'd be the first to acknowledge that his bride-to-be enjoyed spa days, dining at five-star restaurants, and hobnobbing with the rich and famous at chic Hollywood cocktail parties. But there was more to life than fancy soirées and chauffeur-driven limousines. Holding their wedding ceremony in the old barn would give Catherine a taste of the simpler life, the life they were meant to have.

Sarah's arms folded firmly across her body. "Academy Award winner Catherine Mann will not want to get married in an old barn."

That wasn't a reason. That was an opinion. He had a different one. "I think having a wedding out of the spotlight, away from the media, is just what she needs."

It was definitely what he needed. In fact, a simple, private ceremony was the only thing he'd ever asked of Catherine, other than to be his wife. Lately, though, whenever he'd tried to explain how he felt about their special day, he'd gotten the sense that Catherine might have read one too many bridal magazines. He shrugged. He'd gone along when she'd insisted on a destination wedding because, at the time, where they said their vows hadn't mattered to him, as long as they promised to love, honor and cherish one another for the rest of their lives. But things had changed. He'd changed. And, while getting married in a barn might not be Catherine's first choice, she'd always said that compromise was the foundation of a good marriage.

Sarah's hands dropped to her hips. She canted her head. A look of pure disbelief slipped over her features. "Really?"

He was as serious as a heart attack, but he could tell Sarah still needed a little more convincing. The only way to win her over to his side was to broker a deal. "Tell you what," he said, ready to bargain. "I'll help you mend your fence, if you help me plan my wedding."

"Let me see your hands," Sarah demanded.

*My hands?*

She didn't hesitate, but grabbed him by both wrists and tugged his arms toward her. She gave his palms a hard stare. "When was the last time you worked with your hands?"

What was she talking about? He'd spent hours working with his hands every day since he'd plucked out the notes to "Three Blind Mice" on an old flattop he'd found in his uncle's garage. Did he have to point that out to her? From the doubt in her eyes, he guessed he did. "I tour two hundred days out of the year."

"I'm not talking about strumming a guitar." Sarah's firm *humph* declared that his life's work didn't measure up to her needs. She relinquished her grip on his hands. "I need a cowboy for this job."

He had to admit it, he liked seeing her riled up. But it was time to set the record straight. He shook one finger at her. "I am perfectly capable of mending a fence."

"Well, we'll see."

He studied Sarah's raised eyebrows and pursed lips. He'd take that bet and he'd win. "All right."

"I am not getting married in a barn." Beneath the photographer's bright lights, Catherine posed for the cameras. Her veil's silk tulle floated in a lacy cloud around her face.

"He doesn't literally mean an actual barn, does he?" Margaret chose a single kernel from the unsalted, unbuttered popcorn in the bowl while four tuxedo-wearing models took their places around Catherine.

"Yes." Her voice hitched. "He's trying to protect me from the media." She showed the photographer a star-worthy pout while she trailed the tips of her nails across one of the model's chiseled chins. "Offering me a chance to be—" She held the pose.

"Ordinary," Margaret put in.

"Normal," Catherine corrected.

"Why would you want to be normal? Everyone wants to be special. Everyone wants to be you." Margaret lifted the entire bowl of popcorn, squirmed her

Pilates-toned rear onto a director's chair, and grabbed a handful of the tasteless treat.

"I love that he's trying to help me have a normal life." She could almost picture the life Bradley wanted for them, living in some small town so far off the beaten path that the media would never find them and quickly forget them. *Thanks, but um, no thanks.* This was more her style, she thought as two of the models cuddled close while the remaining two gazed down in fawning adoration. "He's the most thoughtful man I've ever known." She aimed a haughty look at the camera and held it. The photographer pointed and snapped. "He's planning everything himself. He's ordering flowers and a cake."

The photographer signaled the models, who swooped her into their arms.

Catherine pointed one of her crystal-studded sandals skyward beneath the layers of the gossamer gown. "His childhood best friend is going to marry us." She relaxed into four pairs of muscled arms, a sated expression on her face. "How lucky am I?"

Shock sent worry lines rippling across Margaret's forehead. "So, what are you going to do?"

"Great. Beautiful, beautiful," the photographer called. Like well-rehearsed dancers, the models adjusted their positions.

"Well, I need to finish shooting this movie." Catherine took advantage of the short break while the photographer checked the light levels. "And he's writing music for the first time in months, so everything'll be fine." The camera lifted toward her. She automatically cupped one of the model's faces in her hands and leaned in close.

"Give it to me."

Twisting to show her slim neck to full advantage, she let her head tip back.

"Beautiful."

Catherine pursed her lips. In between shots, she explained, "I'll go to Texas after we wrap. I'll get married in the barn." She made eye contact with one of the models long enough for the photographer to capture the image. "It'll be a perfect, sweet moment filled with wonderful memories that we'll cherish forever." Pulling herself erect, she brightened. "Then, we'll go to Italy for our one-of-a-kind, amazing wedding."

*Oh!* She got goose bumps just thinking about it.

# Chapter Seven

Aware that the sun had risen above the barn's roofline, Bradley hustled across the grassy field. In the distance, Sarah was already hard at work hammering nails into a wooden slat. Just watching her stirred a painful awareness. After mending fences from sun up to sundown the day before, he'd hurt in places he didn't even know he had muscles. He'd been so tired when Sarah had finally called it a day that he'd limped back to the house and passed out on the bed still wearing his torn and sweat-stained clothes. Today, he'd woken, stiff and sore and hungry enough to eat a horse. The breakfast he'd cobbled together would get him through another day. His clothes were another story. He'd taken one look at his ruined Italian loafers and had thrown them in the trash bin. It had taken some time to search the house for more suitable work clothes, but he'd finally found what he needed in a box of his dad's things in the attic. Tugging on a pair of old work gloves, he hoped Sarah would agree that the wait had been justified. When she propped both hands on a fence board as he approached, he stood cowboy straight and tall.

"Nice boots," she said after sizing up his new look.

"They were my dad's."

The approval that widened Sarah's trademark smile caught him off-guard and sent his gaze straight down to his shoes. The beat-up work shoes bore the stains of a thousand days of pitching hay and shoveling manure. In L.A. or Nashville, his associates would rather die than be caught dead wearing them, but he wasn't trying to impress anyone with fancy clothes or fine footwear in Mill Town. There was real work to be done here. He hefted one of the new boards from a nearby stack. His back protested with a sharp twinge. Aware that Sarah was still watching him, he grunted past the pain.

"All right. Let's get to work."

"He was a good man." Sarah anchored her end of the board in place. "You fill his boots well."

"Thanks."

"He'd be real proud of you." She spoke over her shoulder.

The compliment warmed him more than the thick, cotton shirt he'd pulled from a box in the attic. Heat crawled up his neck. Not sure why her opinion mattered as much as it did, he shot a quick glance at Sarah in time to see an odd expression flash across her face. What was that all about?

He opened his mouth to ask, but she hefted her hammer. Without another word, she drove a nail home with one blow. Not to be outdone, he did the same at the other fence post. He stole a second glimpse of the brunette, noted the way her tool belt hugged her frame, the thick fall of hair that cascaded from her ponytail. A man could do a lot worse than Sarah Standor, and he wondered at the idiocy of the guy who'd let her get away.

He cleared his throat. Sarah's love life was none of his business. Her fence, though, was another matter, and if he wanted her help in planning his wedding, he'd better do less wool-gathering and more hammering.

By sunset, they'd fixed about a mile of fence. Bradley peeled his gloves away from his hands and winced. Despite the gloves, a large blister stretched across the pad of his left hand.

Bradley studied the open tackle box on Sarah's kitchen table. Instead of fishing hooks and line, bandages and creams filled an array of small compartments. Tools and instruments crowded the roomier levels. He tipped his head, uncertain whether he should be impressed by the neatly organized first aid kit or concerned that he'd agreed to let a veterinarian treat his bruises and blisters. His hands were his livelihood. Together with his voice, they'd made him a household name. What if he got an infection? Or worse?

When Sarah turned away from the sink, where she'd spent the last sixty seconds scrubbing her arms and fingers like a surgeon preparing for an operation, his doubts slid away. As a kid, he'd trusted Sarah enough to marry her. If anything, he had more confidence in this grownup version of his pretend wife than he'd had back then.

"Okay, this might sting a bit," she said, sliding onto the chair next to him. She unscrewed the cap on a bottle of alcohol. The acrid smell stung his nose when she poured some on a Q-tip. Leaning in, she dabbed the first of many blisters.

"Yeeoww!" Bradley sucked a sharp breath through his teeth.

"Sorry." Sarah jerked away from his palm.

"Aww, I was just kiddin'." He laughed. "It's fine. Go ahead."

Sarah tsked but went back to work. While she tended to a tiny cut, she said, "You know, you did real good today."

"Thanks." The simple praise sent warmth spreading through his chest. Sarah hadn't been kidding when she'd said that mending fences was hard work. It had taken all his strength to haul the heavy wooden slats out to the fence line. He'd had his doubts that he'd last through a second day of hammering the boards in place. But, aware of how badly he needed Sarah's help to plan his wedding, he'd kept at it. By the end of the day, he was glad he had. The job had given his muscles a better workout than he'd ever gotten in the gym. Besides, it felt good to do real, physical labor for a change.

"Guess you celebrities have people who do all your heavy lifting for you?"

She was closer to the truth than she realized. Back when he was struggling to get his first big break, he hadn't minded handling all his own equipment, lugging the heavy speakers and sound boards around the stage, running the wires, testing the mics. But once he'd "made it," Catherine had insisted that real stars waited to walk onto the set until the crew had everything in place. They left the stage immediately after their performance, she'd coached. He knew she was right. She'd been in the limelight her entire life, after all. Still, he'd missed working alongside the rest of the crew.

"Oh, yeah." He exhaled a breath. Though he'd achieved far more than he'd ever thought possible, he'd found that success came with a whole host of new challenges. He still hadn't figured out how to feed his fans' and the record company's hunger for new material when he was constantly on the road. Touring with the band meant performances that stretched late into the night, catching a few hours' sleep in a hotel room that looked the same as the one the night before, then boarding the bus that didn't stop until they reached the next venue. But he knew better than to complain. Sarah would only tease him if he did. He managed a wry smile instead. "I usually have my butlers do my fence mendin'."

"Ohhhh. Yeah, well, I gave my staff the night off." Sarah took rolls of gauze and tape from the tackle box.

"Otherwise they'd be here just a cookin' and cleanin'. Brushing my hair for me." She swept her ponytail over one shoulder.

He liked the way she giggled when she teased him. It made him feel accepted and welcome in a way he didn't get from either his fans or the people who worked for him. He watched closely as she applied a thick pad over his blisters and wrapped gauze around his hand. "You know, you're pretty good at this."

"Well, I paid enough to learn how to do it." She finished taping the bandage in place. "You're wearing good gloves tomorrow, okay?"

"Yes, ma'am." He flexed his fingers. Thanks to the salve Sarah had used on his hands, the raw skin no longer stung, but a new pair of gloves was definitely in order.

Sarah took a moment to admire her handiwork. "All better," she declared.

"Back in business," he agreed, although it was probably a good thing he didn't plan on performing for a crowd any time soon.

"Let me make you some dinner."

He shook his head as she rose and headed for the stove. He'd never known anyone quite like Sarah. The woman worked had worked as hard as—or harder than—him today. She'd put herself through veterinary school, ran a boarding facility for horses, maintained a world-class garden, and she cooked, too. She was the whole, jean-wrapped package, curves and all. So why on earth was she still single?

"What say we go into town tomorrow? We can knock a few items off your list of wedding preparations." Sarah pulled a frying pan from a cupboard and placed it on the stove.

The idea sounded good to him. He hadn't really taken any time to look around Mill Town since he'd been back. It'd be nice to see how much things had changed in the thirteen years he'd been gone. Plus, a day away from mending fences would give his hands a chance to heal. He rubbed one corner of the Band-Aid. While they were out, he'd take Sarah's advice and pick up a good pair of work gloves. He had a feeling they'd come in handy.

Sarah folded her hands on the table of the Mill Town Family Diner. She doubted anyone in the crowded restaurant would believe her if she announced that Bradley Suttons had carried a tool box out to her fence line. Or that he'd matched her nail for nail, board for board, wearing his custom-made shirt and fancy Italian loafers.

She gave the man across the table from her a wry smile. She would've bet good money against him showing up for a second day of mending fences. Or the third. Especially not in his daddy's old work clothes and wearing a pair of broken-in work boots. But Bradley had kept up his end of their bargain, and he'd done it without a single complaint, even though she knew those blisters on his hands had stung pretty good.

Which left her with no choice but to honor her end of the deal and help him plan his wedding. A wedding that she feared was absolutely not going to make Catherine Mann happy. No matter how many times Bradley insisted Catherine wanted a simple ceremony, or what they did to spruce up the old barn.

"Hi there." As their waitress stepped to the end of their table, Bradley ducked his head. Sarah tore her gaze away from him and stared up at the waitress, whose blue uniform stretched taut across her ample figure when she pulled a pencil from the bun at the nape of her neck. "What can I get for you folks?"

Sarah grinned at Bradley. Hoping to get through the meal without attracting any attention, he'd asked her to place their order. "Well, we will have two Bradley Suttons sandwiches and two Cokes."

"Do you know he used to live here?" Their waitress scribbled in her pad without taking a single glance at her customers.

Unable to resist teasing Bradley just a little, Sarah quipped, "I heard he used to be married to a local gal."

While Bradley's eyes filled with mock horror, their waitress laughed. "No way!" she exclaimed. "I know everything there is to know about Bradley Suttons, and he never married." In a voice filled with self-importance, she added, "Now, he is engaged to Miss Catherine Mann." She wove her pencil into her hair. "And, he *loves* a grilled cheese sandwich."

Bradley chuckled when the woman took off for the kitchen.

An answering snicker worked its way between Sarah's lips. "Oh, she's going to kick herself later."

"Yeah." Bradley agreed. He leaned forward and propped his elbows on the table. "Okay, so you're taking care of the flowers."

Despite a few misgivings, her head bobbed. "Mmm-hmm."

"Now, we need a cake and some music and…"

She stopped him long enough to fight down a serious case of jitters that rose whenever she let herself think about planning her favorite actress's wedding. If they had any hope at all of impressing one of Hollywood's A-List, she'd need to get every detail perfect. "What is Catherine's favorite flower?"

Bradley's lips thinned, and a tiny divot appeared between his eyebrows. "I don't—I don't know."

That made no sense. Even her self-absorbed, lying, cheating ex had known which flowers to send to earn her forgiveness. "You don't know your fiancée's favorite flower?"

"I've sent her flowers before. Plenty of times." Letting his voice drop, Bradley leaned in. "But usually my manager handles sending them." He let out a long, slow breath. "And her manager usually receives them for her."

"Well, how romantic." She rolled her eyes. Superstars like Bradley Suttons and Catherine Mann sure did things differently from most normal folks… and not necessarily for the better.

But she couldn't fault him for his choice of sandwiches. When their still-clueless waitress slid their plates onto the table, her stomach gave a happy growl as she took one sniff of the buttery grilled bread, one glimpse of the golden cheese that drizzled between the slices. While they dug into their food, she peppered Bradley about his plans for the wedding and quickly discovered that, though the man's heart was in the right place, he didn't know the first thing about cakes or flowers or decorations.

Well, that was why he'd asked for her help, wasn't it?

At Appledorn's a little while later, Bradley stared at the array of fancy cakes in the window like someone who'd never stepped foot inside a bakery before. "So, uh, which one do you like?"

Sarah grinned. Bradley had tucked his hands in his pockets, a move she'd seen him make whenever he felt ill at ease. He really was out of his element, wasn't he? "I really like it when they've got flowers all over them, and that way, everybody gets a little flower with their piece of cake." She eyed a chocolate layer cake covered in white fondant, ribbons, and flowers. That one would almost do the trick. She stopped and gave herself a firm reminder that they were here to help Bradley plan his wedding, not hers. "What's Catherine's favorite flavor?"

"I don't really know." Bradley's lips twisted into a wry grimace. "She never really orders dessert."

"Well, no. Of course she doesn't." Sarah cringed

inwardly. She should have known. Someone like Catherine would never binge on sweets. She'd be too afraid of gaining weight. Everyone said the cameras added at least ten pounds. Okay, so the flavor didn't matter, but there were other ways to choose a cake. "What's her favorite color?"

"I'm not exactly sure." The furrows in Bradley's brow deepened until he offered a hesitant, "She wears a lot of black."

"Wait. You don't know your fiancée's favorite flower, favorite flavor, *or* favorite color?" She folded her arms. What was going on here? Either Catherine was extremely private about her likes and dislikes, or Bradley hadn't bothered to learn much about the woman he said he loved. She searched his face for a satisfactory explanation, but reddening slightly, the man stared at the tips of his shoes like a guy who knew he'd done something wrong.

His hangdog expression melted her heart, and she backed off. Bradley and Catherine had only announced their engagement a couple of weeks ago. They'd have a lifetime to discover each other's likes and dislikes. She gave his shoulder a sympathetic tap while she offered some friendly advice. "Well, you'd better find out."

Spotting the owner of the bakery at the display case, she left Bradley to ponder the cakes in the window while she wove a path between small tables to the back of the shop. "Hey Monica. We're going to need a cake for a wedding."

Beneath a mop of blonde hair, Monica's face lit up like fireworks on the Fourth of July.

"You finally decided to settle down." Quickly, she slid a lemon meringue pie onto a glass shelf. Hustling out from behind the case, she propped her fisted hands at her waist. The ruffles on her apron shimmied. "Well, who's the lucky—" Instant recognition dawned in Monica's brown eyes as Bradley turned away from the window. The baker's lips moved, but no sound came out while she stared at the man who crossed the room to stand beside Sarah. At last, her voice hollow, she whispered, "Cake?"

"Yep. Cake." Sarah waved one hand between Bradley and the shop owner. "'Cause that's what you do here. Right, Monica?"

Whatever spell had had its hold on the baker, it broke. She grabbed the hem of her apron and twisted it between her fingers. Her shocked expression deepened into a silly grin the likes of which Sarah had never seen on her friend's face in all the years they'd known each other. "Yes, of course. We do cakes."

"Good. 'Cause Bradley is gonna need a cake. For his wedding." She pointed to the country star, who didn't help matters much by turning up the wattage on his signature smile.

"I am so happy for you and Catherine," Monica blurted. "I think y'all are perfect for each other." She cupped one hand around her mouth and leaned in to share a secret. "I always knew you'd be famous. So..." She clapped her hands. Striding toward a large white board, where delivery dates crowded a hand-drawn calendar, she grabbed a marker. "When is the big day?"

"June first."

"Whoa. Why, that's only a couple of weeks away." Monica dropped the pen into its tray. Turning to face Bradley again, she firmed her jaw. "But for you, I'll make it work."

"Thank you, Monica." Bradley's voice carried such sincerity that the baker blushed. He pointed toward the largest cake in the display window. "I'll take the coconut."

Sarah felt her eyes widen when Monica stumbled back as if Bradley had struck her. She watched as her friend pressed one hand to her chest.

"You can't have that one!" the baker exclaimed. "Catherine Mann is allergic to coconut."

"She is?" Bradley's eyes narrowed while his brows hiked.

"She said so on *The Tonight Show*." Monica shrugged. "Two years ago."

"Okaayy. No coconut."

Now that was interesting. From Bradley's reaction, he'd clearly been in the dark about Catherine's allergy. Sarah tucked a stray wisp of hair behind her ear. How was it possible that ordinary fans like Monica knew more about his bride than Bradley did?

"So." Monica's grin lit up her entire face. In her excitement, she pressed fisted hands to her cheeks. Her voice climbed an octave. "How many layers do we want?"

"I don't know." Bradley stole a quick glance at the cakes in the window. "Two?" he suggested.

Sarah ran the numbers through her head when the groom-to-be glanced her way. The sheet cakes she ordered for Wednesday night church suppers fed fifty with a few slices left over. She nodded. Two layers should do the trick.

"Just two," Monica echoed while disappointment filled her brown eyes.

The baker's glum expression brightened when Bradley tried again. "Make that four," he suggested.

Four. Sarah nodded again. Four was also good. And, while a four-layer cake decorated with white butter cream frosting and fresh flowers was still a far cry from the towering, gold-foiled, fondant-draped edifice she was certain someone like Catherine would expect, Bradley's choice was an excellent one for the down-home wedding he wanted.

# Chapter Eight

Fog still drifted across the valley when Sarah carried her coffee to the window the next morning. A smile tugged at the corners of her mouth while she watched Bradley practice his riding skills in the paddock near the barn. From country music star to wedding planner to horseman, the man accomplished whatever he set his mind to. She'd give him that. She didn't know many men who possessed his tenacity and drive, and, she had to admit, she admired those traits in him.

While he coaxed his horse to back up along the fence, she went over her plans for the day. Like any other morning on the ranch, there were animals to feed, stalls to clean. The florist in town had sent over a special order. She'd fill it before the dew dried on the roses. While she was in town making the delivery, she'd pick up another load of lumber for the fences. She and Bradley would put that to good use this afternoon.

And she needed to check on the status of her grant. In the bakery yesterday, she'd nearly choked when Bradley had announced his wedding date. Of all the days in a year, why had he chosen to get married on the very day she might lose her ranch?

She crossed her fingers. Maybe Bradley's wedding would bring them both the good fortune they needed. Surely, a man who knew as little about his fiancée's likes and dislikes was going to need as much luck as he could get. As for herself, another call to the Equine Rehabilitation Fund was in order. This time, she'd borrow on Bradley's tenaciousness and refuse to give up until she got the answer she wanted.

"No, I don't want to leave another message. I just—"

On the other end of the line, the receptionist cut her off. "I'm sorry," came the voice of a stranger who didn't sound at all sorry. "I'm the only one in the office today. Now, do you want to leave a message or not?"

"Okay, fine." She sighed and shifted the armload of freshly cut flowers while she mounted the steps to the house. Cracking the screen door open wide enough to slip inside, she strode to the kitchen where she added jonquils and roses to an array of hyacinths on the table. "Please tell him Sarah Standor called...again. I'm still waiting to hear if I got the Equine Rescue Grant." Tempted to leave it at that, she borrowed from Bradley's stubborn insistence. It was up to her to make sure the foundation knew her situation was dire. She straightened and pressed the phone closer to her ear. "The bank's gonna foreclose on my property in about two weeks. I got eighteen horses who won't have any-where to go—"

"All that information is in your application, Ms. Standor," came the disembodied voice. "I'll tell him you called. That's all I can do."

"Okay." Frustrated, Sarah struck the table with the flat of her hand. The receptionist was only doing her job. Arguing would only make things worse. But no one seemed to care that, without the Foundation's grant, she'd lose her ranch...and soon. "Okay, yeah," she repeated. "Thank you."

She took a deep breath and tried to relax. When that didn't work the way she wanted it to, she studied the three dogs who'd sprawled across her couch. She could usually count on their sweet faces to make her forget her troubles, but not today. Today, nothing could quell the sense of dread that filled her chest.

Despite a calendar that edged from spring into summer, a bracing chill filled the air as Bradley slid a half-dozen 2x4's from the stack of lumber in the back of Sarah's truck. He eyed her where she stood waiting her turn at the other side of the tail gate. Though Sarah put everything she had into the job, repairing her fences was an all but impossible job for one person. How did she manage when he wasn't around to lend a hand? Giving in to his curiosity, he asked, "You like living on a ranch all alone?"

"I'm not alone." Sarah grabbed another stack of

2x4's from the truck. "I've got my horses and my dogs and my flowers."

He glanced over his shoulder. Horses and dogs made good company, but they couldn't swing a hammer or change a light bulb. Sarah's flowers filled the air with good smells, but they couldn't keep her warm at night. Crossing to a section where every cross piece needed to be replaced, he dropped the load of wood on the ground. "Is that enough?"

For one long second, Sarah stared at the cloudless sky. "No." Sighing, she dumped her slats on the growing pile. "But I want what my parents have, and that doesn't come along every day." Her chin jutted out like it did when she'd been a kid and determined to get her own way.

"Ah, true love." He grabbed another armload.

"Oh, come on." Sarah's mouth dropped open. "You don't believe in true love?"

*Why would I? Doesn't love always end in heartbreak?*

He thought about all the people and things he'd ever loved. His parents. Friends like Sarah and Adam. His life here in Mill Town. One terrible accident had ripped them all away from him. He shook his head. He and Catherine shared something far more practical, something Sarah clearly didn't understand. He supposed he ought to explain it to her. He owed her that much. "I think you find someone you care about, someone whose company you enjoy, who likes the same things you like, wants the same things you want." With the truck unloaded, he rested one hip on the tailgate and peeled off his gloves. "After that, it's hard work and compromise."

Sarah propped one hand on the quarter panel and cocked a hip. "I want someone who's gonna love me forever, no matter what. Who wants to walk through life leaning up against me so neither one of us falls."

"Well, that sounds real romantic." There'd been a time when he'd believed in knights in shining armor who rescued the fair maidens and lived happily ever after. His parents' deaths had put an end to such flights of fancy. "But not very realistic." He'd learned from that harsh lesson.

"I agree, it is rare." Sarah grabbed her tool belt from the back of the truck. Lost in thought, she added, "Plus, you only get one shot at it. And even then, you've got to be in the right place to recognize it. And choose it. And fight for it." Wrapping the thick leather strap around her, she snagged the belt tight.

"So this, uh, *magical* relationship." He stood. "It only happens once in a lifetime?"

"Yep."

"And you got to be in the right place. At the right time. Or you miss it?" No wonder Sarah hadn't found her Prince Charming. Even she had to realize how badly the odds were stacked against her.

"Yep."

He cinched his own tool belt around his waist and grabbed his gloves. "I think you've read too many romance novels." What Sarah was describing only existed in books and sappy country songs.

"Maybe." Sarah shook her head as she walked away. "But I'm not gonna settle for less."

Bradley slipped his fingers into the pair of heavy-duty gloves he'd picked up at the hardware store on their excursion into town the day before. "Well, I hope you get your happily ever after," he said while Sarah wrestled a rotted slat out of the fence. "You deserve it."

Even without the full moon to light his path, Bradley could have followed the tantalizing odor of food cooking over an open fire. Through the trees, he spotted Sarah kneeling at the edge of a campfire.

"Now why'd you bring me all the way out here?" he asked when he got close enough.

"Well." Sarah finished adjusting what looked like fresh-caught trout on a spit. "You've been working so hard, I thought we'd take a night off and go to the movies."

"The movies?" He peered into the darkness. Bushes and trees surrounded them. Here and there, rocks jutted out of the earth, but none of them were big enough for a movie screen. Besides, no extension cord could possibly reach from here to the house. What kind of show could they watch without a projector?

"Cowboy style," she added, as if that detail explained anything. Using a rock for a pillow, Sarah stretched out on the ground. "Lie back."

"All right." If Sarah wanted to pretend to watch movies, he'd play along. The Stetson he swept from his head gleamed white as the moon in the night air. To keep it clean, he anchored the hat on his chest while he propped his shoulders against a small boulder.

"This is one of my favorites." Staring up, Sarah squirmed just enough to get comfortable. "It stars the Big and Little Dipper in one of their best adventures."

Tipping his head to the sky, Bradley let the tension of the last few days flow off his shoulders. Majestic pines pointed upward where, against the inky backdrop, tiny pinpoints of light shone brightly. In an instant he was awash in memories of summer nights when he and Sarah and Adam had camped out under the stars in the backyard. "I love this movie. I remember watching it when I was a kid."

"This is the sequel."

He laughed at Sarah's dry delivery. That was one thing he really liked about her, he thought as he stared up at the sky. She seemed to find the humor in everything. Take this afternoon when he'd tackled the massive job of cleaning out the barn for the wedding. There hadn't been anything fun about toting bales of hay, sweeping, and washing the floors. But then, Sarah had doused him with her hose, a move that had led to an epic water fight that had raged off and on while they'd laughed and scoured the barn from the rafters to the floorboards. Under normal circumstances, all that hard, sweaty work would have been sheer drudgery. But Sarah had turned it into the most fun he'd had in ages. He'd have to remember to thank her for it before he left town.

When a few clouds scuttled across the sky and hid the stars, Sarah rose to check on the fish roasting over the fire. After adjusting the spit, she turned to face him. The flickering flames cast a rosy glow on her cheeks. "You know, I've been listening to you play your new songs at night. They sound real good. They remind me a lot of the ones you wrote when you were first startin' out. You know, take you on a journey. Make you feel somethin'." As if she thought she'd said too much, she poked at the embers with a stick.

Bradley blinked slowly. Until he'd come home to Mill Town, he'd failed so miserably at creating the meaningless but upbeat songs the record executives wanted that he'd started questioning his ability ever write a good song again. But Sarah's praise could mean that he was back on track. "You really think so?" Leaning forward, he held his breath, waiting for an answer.

"Well, why would I say it if it wasn't true?" Sarah crossed one arm over the other and stared at him like he'd lost his mind.

He sighed. He'd spent so much time in Nashville and Los Angeles, he'd nearly forgotten what it was like to hang out with someone who made honesty and directness two of their watchwords. "The world I live in is full of people who tell me what they think I want to hear." His agent, the record executives, his assistant, even Catherine—they peppered him with praise. Even when, a lot of the time, he knew he didn't deserve it.

"Well, I'll never do that."

"Good." The earnestness that shone in Sarah's eyes made a refreshing change from his life in the city. He pulled himself into a sitting position and centered the Stetson on his head.

Sarah leaned in close enough to whisper. "So, can I tell you something? Truthfully?"

"Yeah, sure."

"That hat." The corners of her lips pulled her mouth into a frown.

*Uh-oh.* Whatever Sarah had to say about the expensive Stetson, he was pretty sure he wouldn't like it. He groaned and braced for the worst. "What about it?"

"Well, you think it makes you look like a cowboy, but..." Sarah's voice trailed off.

"I love this hat, okay? It's new." He heard the defensive note in his tone and tamped it down. "My manager, Hank, sent it to me for my tour."

"Well, that's your problem. A real cowboy would never wear a new hat." Sarah snatched the offensive object from his head. Her movements quick and sure, she smashed the crown into the dirt.

"Hey! What are you doing?" he asked, although the answer seemed perfectly clear.

She kept smashing and grinding it into the ground. When she finally finished, sand rained down on his shirt as she plopped the considerably darker, misshapen hat on his head with a self-satisfied, "There. That's better."

"Oh, man." Maybe he should rethink that whole

honesty thing. Almost afraid to look at what she'd done, he took the ruined Stetson from his head. Dark smudges marred the once-pristine felt. The smooth brim had been transformed into a wavy line. Although his agent would probably have a conniption, he had to admit, Sarah's modifications gave the hat character.

# Chapter Nine

Armed with a list of stops to make and supplies to gather for the wedding, Bradley scanned Mill Town's Main Street through the passenger window of Sarah's truck. The awnings that offered protection from snow and sleet over the long winters now shaded weekday shoppers from bright sunshine. Birds billed and cooed from nests in the mature trees that lined the town's sidewalks. Enjoying the warm weather, customers slowly browsed through Mom-and-Pop shops that offered everything from dresses to kitchen supplies. Pickup trucks and late-model sedans filled most of the slant-in parking spots. Something about the decided lack of limos and Town Cars put a spring in his step as he bounded from the front seat. He gave a contented sigh and glanced at the woman who rounded the front bumper. "You know, this was a good place to grow up."

"Well, I'm glad you remember that." The heels of her dress boots tapped sharply on the asphalt. Sarah paused to stare down a passerby who'd stopped to gape at them. When the other person moved on, the hem of her skirt fluttered about her knees as she strode briskly across the street. "Have you and Catherine talked about where you want to settle down and raise your children?"

Bradley tucked his hands into the pockets of his jeans. Whenever he was with Catherine, they were usually surrounded by people—her agent or his, their assistants, the paparazzi. And that was before his bride-to-be had announced their engagement on national TV. Since then, they hadn't had a moment's privacy. They certainly hadn't had a chance to make long-term plans. "I don't know if Catherine wants to have children."

"Do you?"

"Sure." Aware that people were stopping to stare and a few had aimed cell phones in his direction, he kept his answer short and to the point. But, yeah, he'd dreamed of having a family for almost as long as he could remember. A little boy with a crooked smile. Or a girl with wavy brown curls.

"Wait. What?" A mix of confusion and doubt played across the face that stared up at him. "You're getting married, but you haven't discussed whether you want a family?" Sarah tsked. "Celebrities are an odd breed."

"I am not a celebrity." Stardom was more Catherine's thing. Sure, he'd dreamed of the day when eager fans would snap up tickets to his concerts so fast they'd sell out in one day, or when journalists and reporters would seek him out. But now that the accolades and awards poured in, more and more he relished times like these when he could just be himself.

"Yes, clearly." Sarah gestured toward the faces of the other shoppers who were failing miserably at pretending not to stare.

Bradley painted a canned smile on his face. His appearance in town had attracted some attention, but he'd learned a few tricks from Catherine about handling nosy fans. He and Sarah would just have to duck into a store for a while, and people would quickly lose interest. He swept the area for a likely spot. His gaze caught on a sign for Stucky's Candy and Ice Cream. "I love this place," he announced. Squaring around to face Sarah, he recalled the countless times they'd ridden their bikes into town for ice cream on hot summer afternoons. "Mint chip, right?"

"Very good."

The way her lips parted told him how surprised she was that he'd recalled her favorite flavor. He grabbed her hand and hustled her down the street. Hand in hand, they dashed into a storefront so narrow, it barely provided enough room for two in front of the display case that ran the length of the tiny store. Once they'd crossed the threshold, he firmly shut the door while, on the sidewalk outside, a few determined souls called for autographs and pictures. But by the time they emerged with their cones a scant fifteen minutes later, he and Sarah had the sidewalk to themselves. He made a note to thank Catherine for showing him the trick next time they spoke and turned his attention to the rich blend of hand-churned ice cream that was every bit as good as he remembered from his childhood.

"Our next stop is Mill Town Bridal," Sarah announced between bites of green mint dotted with chunks of dark chocolate. "How many guests are you thinking of having?"

"I hadn't thought about it." He took another swipe at his cone while he reviewed the list of people he saw on a daily basis when he was at home in Nashville. He wasn't close enough to any of them to actually invite them to his wedding. "I work with a lot of people, but I don't have a lot of time to socialize." He hated the pitying look the comment earned him but shrugged it aside. Friendships took time to develop, and time was always in short supply.

At the bridal shop, Sarah lingered in front of the window, where a mannequin was decked out in a confection of lace and chiffon. Her eyes shimmered. "I bet she's got some fancy designer making her a gown," she said, her voice wistful.

"You're probably right." Though he'd repeatedly asked Catherine to keep the fuss for their wedding down to a minimum, he doubted she'd buy a dress off the rack. His bride-to-be probably wouldn't even glance at the price tag on the gown she'd only wear for a few hours.

Slowly, he licked his ice cream. He had to admit that Sarah was right about something else, too—the next time he saw Catherine, they needed to have a serious talk…about so many things. Children. Where they'd live. How they'd handle finances. Thanks to his recent success, he'd never have to worry about money again for the rest of his life, but he'd scrimped and scraped through enough lean years that he didn't enjoy tossing his money away willy-nilly. That was another thing he shared in common with Sarah.

He squeezed his eyes tight while tiny doubts nibbled at his thoughts. In the days he'd been away from L.A., he'd stayed so busy that he hadn't missed Catherine. At least, not nearly as much as he thought he would. Or should. Of course, planning their wedding took up a lot of his time, but he couldn't help but wonder if doing something *for* someone was as important as spending time *with* them. What if, when they did finally get together, he and Catherine couldn't resolve their differences?

He shook the idea right out of his head. He and his fiancée had the same dreams, the same goals. They respected one another. They'd make their marriage work. He swallowed, and the last cold bit of cream cooled the back of his throat.

"C'mon." Sarah's warm smile broke into his reverie with a reminder that they'd come to town today on a mission. She tugged on the crook of his arm. "Let's get you a tuxedo."

"All right."

He supposed it wasn't every day that a Grammy winner walked into the Mill Town Bridal Store. Within minutes, he stood on a raised platform in front of a three-way mirror while a star-struck sales clerk smoothed a tiny wrinkle from the best tux in the house. Bradley ran a hand down the pleated shirt and straightened the bow tie. The black wool number definitely fit the bill for a country wedding in a barn on the outskirts of town.

From beyond the edge of the mirror, Sarah chimed, "Well, you are going to make a very fancy groom."

The outfit wasn't bad, but he couldn't shake the feeling that he'd overlooked something. "Yeah, I don't know," he said to the clerk. "Something doesn't feel right."

"You know, you're right." Sarah pointed a finger. "Something is missing." She stepped down from the raised platform and crossed to a hat rack near the cash register. Returning quickly, she plopped a black cowboy hat on his head. "There. Now, you're all set."

Bradley adjusted the brim to a rakish angle that added the perfect dash of spice to the outfit. "Oh, yeah." He slipped the jacket's single button through its hole. "Now I feel good," he announced. Wearing a wide grin, he gave Sarah a mock salute and enjoyed the sound of her laughter.

As much as Sarah hated to admit it, seeing Bradley in a tux turned a flock of butterflies loose in her chest. She steeled herself against the feeling. Star or no star, she had no business going all gooey-eyed over the man. Bradley wasn't the kid next door anymore. While she struggled to hold on to her family's ranch, he'd grown up and moved on. He'd overcome major hurdles that would have destroyed anyone who had less drive or talent and was fast on his way to becoming a legend in the country music industry. If all that wasn't enough to keep them apart, in less than two weeks, he'd marry Catherine Mann.

Although, if she had to put her finger on the problem, that was it, wasn't it? How could he marry someone he knew so little about? He didn't even know his fiancée's favorite flower. Yet he'd recalled her own love for mint chocolate, and they hadn't been around each other for a very long time. Of course, he said Catherine never ate dessert, so maybe she'd never mentioned her allergy to coconut, just like she'd never told him if she preferred chocolate over strawberry, lemon over lime.

But…children. How could he be completely in the dark over whether or not Catherine wanted children? Or, if she did, where she wanted to settle down to raise them? Sarah had never known anyone who considered themselves in love enough to get married but didn't know anything about the person they'd spend the rest of their lives with.

It certainly didn't sound as if Catherine and Bradley had the forever kind of love she insisted on finding before she tied the knot. Then again, she guessed that was his business.

Just like it was her business to support him no

matter what. 'Cause that was what friends did for one another.

"Do you have your dress yet?"

Sarah tore her gaze from Bradley to face the saleswoman who'd walked up behind her. Her cheeks warming, she stared into the face of a kindly looking matron. "Oh, no. No. I'm just—"

"Don't say another word," commanded the woman, whose French twist was as much a part of her working uniform as the white gloves she wore when she handled the bridal gowns. "I have the perfect dress for you."

"Well, I—" Sarah cast a pleading look at Bradley, but the man and the tailor were deep into a discussion of cuff versus no cuff. No help there. Not wanting to appear rude, she surrendered to the clerk's insistent tug on her arm.

Besides, she reasoned, why not take advantage of the opportunity to try on a dress or two? With no boyfriend in sight—much less a fiancé—she might never get the chance again.

As she stepped into the dressing area, her gaze narrowed in on the single gown the saleswoman had hung from a hook in a curtained alcove. The butterflies that had settled in her stomach took flight again the moment she took in the dress's simple lines and uncluttered look. Blinking, she glanced at the sales clerk. How had the woman sized her up in the short time she and Bradley had been in the store? No matter. She made quick work of shucking her everyday clothes and slipping her fingers through armholes. The lace-trimmed front cascaded down over her knees to the floor in a waterfall of satin.

"This tiny mirror isn't big enough to get the full effect," the saleswoman declared while she zipped Sarah into the dress. "Let's go out to the three-way so you can see how it really looks." From seemingly out of thin air, she produced a pair of elegant white sandals, which slid smoothly onto Sarah's bare feet.

Moving as if she was in a dream, Sarah made her way to the viewing platform in the center of the store. The salesclerk was right again, she decided as she stared at her own reflection in the large mirror. Rich white satin flared slightly over her hips and fell to the floor in a cascade of lace and flowers. From the simple sleeveless design to the fitted bodice with its modest V-neck, she'd never seen anything so lovely. It was as if the gown had been designed especially for her.

And seeing herself in it, for the first time in her life, she ached for the whole deal. For friends and family crowding the aisles. For the flower girls and the ring bearer. For the minister up front and, most of all, the man she loved at her side. She wanted it all.

She turned to Bradley, who'd left his purchases at the cash register and had made a beeline to the viewing area when she'd stepped out of the dressing room. Tears clogged her throat. She cleared it. "She's right. It's perfect." She made an instant decision. "If I ever do get married, this is the dress I'm going to wear."

His voice thick with emotion, Bradley agreed. "You look like a princess."

*I do, don't I.* She skimmed one hand over the satin.

The sales clerk beamed at them over an armload of veils. "You make a lovely bride and groom."

"Oh, no." Hurrying to correct the woman who'd been so helpful, Sarah waved a finger between her and Bradley. "We're not getting married."

"Not again, anyway," Bradley chimed in. "We got married years ago."

"Oh, I, I see." A look that was one part confusion and two parts concern raised the sales clerk's eyebrows.

"Yep." Bradley propped one heel on the edge of the viewing platform and hitched his belt. "I'm marryin' a new bride."

The hands holding the veils drifted a bit lower while, if anything, the clerk's brows rose higher. "You bring your old bride to the store to try on a dress for your new bride?"

"That's right." Bradley's grin stretched from ear to ear.

"Well!" Her hopes of making a big sale dashed, the clerk moved away while a succession of ever-fading "well, well, well's" trailed in her wake.

Sarah struggled hard against the kind of laughter that could just as quickly dissolve into tears. Bradley's joke was just the thing she'd needed to keep from falling to pieces.

# Chapter Ten

When Sunday rolled around again, Bradley made sure he'd stepped onto Sarah's porch ten minutes before, rather than ten minutes after, the departure time she'd set. Not that it had made any difference. If anything, his presence in Adam's tiny church sent even more shock waves through the congregation than it had the week before. While titters whispered behind him, he sat, his hands clasped in his lap, his eyes forward, just the way his mama had taught him to behave in church. Apparently though, the majority of Adam's parishioners had skipped that lesson.

"Now, God says to love your enemies." From his post at the pulpit, Adam waited for the commotion to die down. When it didn't, he plunged ahead with his sermon. "Now, that has to be one of the hardest commandments on the list."

Bradley winced when a young teen in the choir loft actually aimed a cell phone at him. Pointing and talking in stage whispers, the boy bragged to the other robed singers about the picture he'd taken.

The conversations in the pews had grown so loud, Bradley could barely hear Adam above the hubbub. He drummed his hat on one knee.

As much as he wanted to hear what Adam had to say, perhaps he should leave. That was what Catherine would do. She'd tell him if his presence created this much distraction, he ought to skip church altogether.

"These days, what with the news and internet full of..." Adam aimed a stern frown at the women in the front row who, from all appearances, were paying no attention at all to his sermon. His lips thinned and arrowed down at the corners. "Well, I think what's most important in life is that we all paint our houses purple."

When no one in the congregation so much as blinked, Bradley grinned an apology at his old friend. Meanwhile, beside him, Sarah buried her head in her hands.

"I believe we'd all be better people if we paint our houses purple." Adam's voice rose an octave. "With, um, pink polka dots, too."

"Excuse me." At Sarah's whisper, Bradley braced himself. Before he had a chance to ask what she was up to, she jumped to her feet. "Can I—can I have your attention, ya'll?" Her hands clasped in front of her, she aimed a glance toward the front of the little church. "So sorry, Pastor Adam. I just have an announcement to make."

Around them, the room quieted.

"Bradley Suttons, homegrown country music star—"

Not at all sure where Sarah was going, but willing to follow her lead, Bradley tipped his cowboy hat to the crowd.

"—would like to invite you all to attend his wedding to movie star Catherine Mann."

*Wait. What?* His chin jerked up. He had to have heard Sarah wrong. He stared up at the woman who continued on as if she hadn't just fired a load of buckshot into his plans for a small intimate wedding.

"It's going to be held on June first," she announced. "In my barn. So, until then, let's give Bradley some privacy. And let's get back to Pastor Adam and his beautiful sermon. Okay?"

"Thank you, Sarah." At the podium, Adam pressed one hand to his heart.

Having said her piece, Sarah slipped onto the pew beside him, while Bradley did his best to figure out why on earth his friend would take it upon herself to invite the entire congregation to his wedding. His voice barely able to contain his shock, he swiveled to face her. "You just invited fifty strangers to my wedding."

"They aren't strangers," she whispered back. "Most of 'em have known you since you were a kid, and they all loved you before you were a big star."

*She's a piece of work, that Sarah.*

There were a few choice words he wanted to share with her, but recognizing that this was neither the time nor the place, he forced his attention to the pulpit. In the pews in front of him, cameras had been returned to purses and pockets. No one peered at him over a seat back. No titter of distracting conversation threatened to drown Adam's delivery. For the first time since he'd walked into the church and taken his seat on the wooden pew a little while ago, Bradley heard every word of the sermon.

*Well, I'll be.*

He repositioned his hat on his knee. Catherine had always declared that it was best to ignore or run from unwanted attention. Truth be told, he didn't care for that tactic, because it alienated the very people he was trying so hard to reach—his fans. But Sarah had tried a different approach, and her method of confronting the situation head-on had worked. Especially when she promised them the very thing they wanted—more access to him and Catherine. He'd have to keep that in mind the next time he ventured into town and someone asked for an autograph or picture. And he would, right after he figured out how to deal with the extra guests the girl next door had invited to his wedding.

He was still thinking of how much extra cake and punch he'd need while he sat between Adam and Sarah at their old fishing hole that afternoon.

"It was real nice of you to invite the town to your wedding." Adam unfolded the waxed paper from the sandwich he'd pulled from Sarah's ice chest.

Beside him, Sarah stared to the side with arched

eyebrows. Bradley shifted his weight in the camp chair he'd erected on the rock-strewn bank of the river. He'd had nothing to do with the plan, but if Sarah wanted their friend to think it had all been his idea, he'd play along. He chuckled. "It just seemed like the right thing to do."

Adam munched thoughtfully on his sandwich. "I think being home has been healing for you. Opening your heart will lead to a peaceful life."

Bradley pretended to check the tension on his fishing line while he considered his friend's words. For years, he'd dreaded coming back to Mill Town, having to deal with his parents' death and the feelings he'd buried when they'd died. And, yeah, since he'd been back, he'd felt the loss of his mom and dad more keenly than ever. Every box he unpacked, every picture on the mantle, reminded him of them. But where he'd feared his childhood memories would drag him down, dealing with his past had actually had the opposite effect. He felt more settled, more ready to face the future than ever before. Coming back home had given him the chance to work with Sarah, something he'd enjoyed far more than he'd thought possible. But the thing that shocked him the most was that, away from all the distractions—the parties, the appearances, the endless media ops that couldn't be denied—he was writing again. Really writing. At last count, at least a dozen new songs filled the pages of his notepad. He nodded to Adam. "I think you're right."

"How are the wedding plans coming?" Adam took another bite.

From her seat on his other side, Sarah's fingers tightened around her coffee cup. "Well." She inhaled deeply. "We're done."

Adam chewed and swallowed. "I'm sure looking forward to meeting Catherine. You must love her very much."

"I do." Bradley exhaled. "I do." Out of the corner of his eye, he thought he caught the faintest trace of disapproval darken Sarah's features.

He told himself not to be ridiculous. Sarah had been nothing but cooperative and helpful in making all the arrangements for his wedding. She wouldn't do that if she harbored any doubts about his upcoming marriage, would she? Maybe he should follow the example she set in church this morning and simply confront the situation. He opened his mouth to ask her if she had anything to say, but stopped when a hard tug at the end of his fishing line suddenly demanded his attention.

"Whoa!" He leaped to his feet. Reeling in as fast as he could, he waded knee-deep into the river. Thirty yards upriver, the water boiled with an excited thrashing. The fish was hooked. Now, if he could only keep tension on the line till he got it ashore.

"Ha-ha-ha! There she is," Adam called as a glistening trout broke the surface.

"C'mon, baby," Bradley coaxed. He leaned forward,

willing the fish closer. Water splashed behind him, and he relaxed, knowing Sarah had his back.

"Oh! Oh, that's a big one," she called from just over his shoulder. Giddy with excitement, she laughed and clapped her hands.

Suddenly, the fish was within reach. Shifting the rod to his other hand, Bradley dashed through the shallows after the flash of sparkling fins. The fish shied away, putting as much distance between them as possible. If he could only grab it... He lunged again. His hand closed over wriggling flesh. In the next second, the granddaddy of all trout wiggled from the tips of his outstretched fingers.

"You did it!" Sarah jumped up and down.

Pride and joy bubbled within him. This was a moment that had to be shared. He reached for Sarah, swung her around, and squeezed her tight. When he did, every nerve ending in his body snapped to attention, filling him with an awareness of Sarah's curves. She felt so right in his arms that he couldn't help but hold onto her while he pressed her closer than any friend ever should. The instant he did, he knew he'd made a huge mistake. Heat crawled up the back of his neck. He reacted by quickly setting Sarah back on her feet. Bending low over the fish at the end of his line, he shot the woman a questioning look. Had he ruined things between them?

"Nice work!" she exclaimed, apparently oblivious to his discomfort.

He allowed himself one relieved breath. But

straightening a moment later, Bradley stared straight into Adam's eyes. The minister and third member of their band of musketeers only shook his head, but the slight gesture was enough to convey a wary concern.

Bradley swallowed past a lump in his throat. Sarah was a friend, maybe his best friend. But his feelings for her didn't go any further. He'd made a mistake by hugging her the way he had, but that was all it had been. A simple mistake. A one-time thing. Adam— and he—had nothing to worry about...as long as he made sure it never happened again.

Under clear blue skies, Sarah drove a final nail into the wooden slat. A short distance away, Bradley wrestled a thick wooden post into a freshly dug hole. The job really required two people, and she'd tsked at his stubbornness when he'd insisted on doing it by himself.

What was going on with him? He'd been quiet and withdrawn all morning. To be honest, though, she'd noticed a change in his attitude yesterday. It was as if an invisible barrier had dropped between them the moment they'd celebrated his awesome catch at the fishing hole. The minute he'd let her go, he'd backed away from her like a kid who'd wandered too close to a fire. Nothing had been the same between them since then.

She rubbed her chin. The hug—that had to be the reason for this new and totally unacceptable distance between them. And no wonder. She couldn't speak for Bradley, but that embrace had certainly changed the way she looked at him. Sure, she'd already had a few questions about his relationship with Catherine. No matter how hard she tried to see things differently, she couldn't shake the feeling that Bradley and Catherine were more like business partners than love birds. For his sake, she'd been willing to set aside her doubts, her qualms. But then...

He'd hugged her. And once she'd felt his strong arm around her waist, once she'd pressed her head to his wide chest, it was as if a dam had broken. Suddenly, all the feelings of friendship she'd had for him had morphed into something far deeper, something she'd never, ever act on.

Not as long as he was engaged to someone else.

Not as long as he loved someone else.

Was that the reason for his cool indifference this morning? Was he struggling with a new awareness of her, the same way she fought her feelings for him? If so, they both needed to get over it, and soon. She wasn't foolish enough to think he'd change his plans to marry Catherine Mann. Not over one hug. No matter how good it felt. She didn't want him to, either. She knew what it felt like to be the jilted one. She knew the hurt of discovering that the one you loved had been unfaithful. She'd never put another woman through that pain. Not for her.

She gave her head a firm, thought-clearing shake. In a few days, Bradley and Catherine would marry in her barn. They'd jet off to Europe for their honeymoon. In the future, Bradley would live a life far different from her own struggle-filled days.

Until then, though, she and Bradley had to work together. To do that, they had to move beyond this barrier between them. Wishing they could simply roll back the clock to that fateful moment at the river and undo the damage, she propped one foot on a rail. A short distance away, Bradley shoved a tamper over the fence post and pounded it deeper into the ground. He'd changed a lot in the nearly two weeks they'd been working together. A compliment might go a long way toward healing the breach between them, and she offered one. "You learn fast."

No response.

Her brows knitted. The time had come to try a different approach. While Bradley bent over a shovel, she closed the distance between them. "I think that whole country-star persona is a put-on," she teased. "You're really just a cowboy deep down."

"Well, my dad was." Bradley worked an extra shovel-full of dirt into the hole. "I think that's where my life was headed before he and my mom died."

Okay, so it wasn't fun and games, but at least he was talking to her again. She could work with that. She grabbed an extra spade from a stack of nearby tools and set about shoring up the pole from the opposite side. "Guess we never know what life's going to throw at us, do we?"

"You know, when I moved to Nashville, living in

the city was such a change. I don't think I ever really got used to it." Bradley planted his shovel in the ground.

The wistful tone in his voice twisted her insides. His fans, the people he worked with, his band—she bet all they saw were his good looks and talent. But she knew the real Bradley. The one he hid beneath a cool outer shell. She'd been there when his folks had died, when he was so devastated that it had broken her own heart. Like that day, she ached to reassure him. To let him know he had people he could count on—his neighbors, Adam, her. "Your roots are always your roots."

"You know, I think I forgot what being home is supposed to feel like."

While Bradley leaned against a sturdy fence post, she retrieved a Thermos from their lunch pack. When he'd first come to town, he'd sworn that everything about Mill Town was in his past. Had he changed his mind?

"I spent so much time trying to forget this place." He stared into the distance, where a car drove slowly along the main road skirting the property. "But being back here—with you—it's bringing it all back. This is home."

Her breath caught in her throat. Did he mean he was sticking around? What about his career? His marriage to Catherine? Had he changed his mind about that, too? So many questions crowded her thoughts, she didn't know which one to ask first. Rather than pick the wrong one, she handed him a cup of coffee and waited to hear what he'd say next.

"You know, I don't know why I told you all that." Bradley pushed himself upright. Brushing past her, he propped one hand atop a new section of fence. "I mean, I—I never really talk about this stuff." He stared down at his coffee cup for a long moment before he looked up and met her gaze. "Thank you...for helping me find my way back to who I was."

She sucked in a shuddery breath. She shouldn't be the one who helped Bradley rediscover himself, his roots, where he belonged. That job belonged to his fiancée. She was just his wedding planner, a fact she needed to keep in mind. The time had come to remind him of that, too. Taking the coffee cup from his outstretched hand, she cleared her throat. "You're gonna need music for your wedding."

"Yeah." Bradley retrieved his shovel.

"There's a great band in town." Their old grade school friend, Sammy, sang lead in the country western group that set toes tapping every time they appeared at the Mill Town Corral. "They're playing tomorrow night, if you want to go see them."

"That'd be great."

She took a fortifying sip of coffee while she chewed on the realization that, no matter how much things had changed for Bradley, he was still marrying Catherine Mann. For both their sakes, she needed to put some distance between them. A crowded bar sounded just like what the doctor would order. She'd ask Adam to join them, and the three musketeers would have a few laughs, dance to some music, relive the carefree days of their youth. Best of all, surrounded by friends and neighbors, there'd be no chance of repeating yesterday's warm embrace.

# Chapter Eleven

Night birds called from their nests as Bradley cut across the field to Sarah's house. The tall grass brushed his boots with every step. He aimed a promise at the gate in her picket fence when it swung open with a squeak. Tomorrow. He'd oil the hinges tomorrow. Tonight, there'd be no backbreaking work mending fences, no chores to tackle. Tonight was for music and good times, something that was long overdue. If this were Nashville or L.A., he'd have been out on the town every night, dropping in for a performance at the Bluebird, swinging by the Cowboy Palace to listen to an up-and-coming band. But in the two weeks that had passed since he'd come to Mill Town, he'd lived like a hermit while he worked on the new songs for an album that was coming together very nicely, even if he did say so himself. Still, it'd be good to get out, visit with friends, take a spin across the dance floor. The thought added a little pep to his step as he trotted up the stairs to rap on Sarah's front door.

"Evenin'," he said when she answered.

Stepping onto the porch, Sarah tossed a soft "Hi" over her shoulder while she locked up.

"You all set?" It felt odd, just the two of them heading out for a night on the town. Whenever he and Catherine ventured out together, her entourage of assistants and makeup artists usually accompanied them. To say nothing of the paparazzi who dogged their every step.

"Mm-hum."

He suppressed a low whistle when, trailing a light floral scent in her wake, Sarah's slight figure brushed past him and headed down the stairs. The slicked-back hair she normally wore in a ponytail had been set free to trail in curls around her shoulders. Beneath a snug-fitting denim jacket, her dress pinched in at her waist before falling in soft folds that ended above her knees. Something was off, though. He could feel it. Her answers were too subdued, too cool. Determined to get a rise out of her, he summoned a teasing grin. "You know, you clean up real good for a cowgirl."

"Well, thank you, kind sir." Sarah motioned toward her feet. "These are my Saturday go-to-town boots."

He smiled in return. That was better. That was the Sarah he knew. "Well, let's git." He settled his hat on his head and escorted her to her truck for the short ride into town.

They snagged a parking space just beyond the swinging doors of the Mill Town Corral, where music spilled onto the street. He paused to listen. The cover band Sammy had mentioned when he'd first arrived in town was in full swing…and they weren't half bad. In fact, they were every bit as good as many of the bands whose music filled the airways. The drummer measured out an up-tempo beat that had a fair-sized crowd on its feet. On the dance floor, couples two-stepped while fiddles sawed and guitars twanged. Following Sarah's lead, he headed inside, where he nodded hello to the band leader on bass, then followed quickly on the heels of Sarah's boots when she cut a path through the crowded bar to the spot where Adam had saved seats for them.

"Hey! How are ya?"

His stomach gave an unexpected shimmy when Sarah stepped into Adam's welcoming embrace. Surprised by how difficult it became to keep his trademark smile in place, he extended his hand as Sarah stepped aside. "How ya doin', Adam?"

"You two going to twirl around the floor?" Taking Sarah's jacket and purse, Adam set them on one of the stools he'd reserved.

"Maybe after a few." For now, he just wanted to soak in the atmosphere and listen to music from the band that would probably play at his wedding. Around them, people clapped and cheered when a rocking instrumental drew to a close.

"Thank you!" Sammy called while waitresses wove between tables taking orders and delivering drinks. He strummed the opening bars of their next number, a slow ballad guaranteed to put even the most stalwart cowboy in the mood.

Over Adam's shoulder, Bradley swept a glance through the crowd. A bearded fellow cupped his hands over his wife's swollen belly and drew the expectant mom toward him. They swayed in time with the music. Around the room, couples paired off while Sammy crooned a love song.

"It's good—the slow music." Sarah spoke above the sawing fiddle, the rattle of glassware, the sound of boots and shoes shuffling against the wooden floor. "'Cause you're gonna need romantic dancin' music, too."

She was right, as usual. He'd never been to a wedding where the DJ didn't spin at least a half-dozen slow songs. He glanced down at Sarah. After a full day of mucking stalls, mending fences, and handling a thousand other tasks, she'd taken pains with her clothes and hair and driven into town, just so he could choose a band to play at his wedding. After all that, she deserved a swing or two around the dance floor. Hoping Adam might offer, he searched for their friend. But Adam had slid onto a bar stool where he sat, lost in the music while he nursed a tall glass of ice tea. Which, he supposed, left him to do the honors.

He extended a hand. "You want to dance?"

"Yeah. Okay." Sarah's curls shimmied when she nodded her head. "You dance?" she asked, gliding into his arms.

"I try." Their shared laughter floated in the space between them. "Okay, are you ready?" he asked when they'd taken a couple of turns. "'Cause I'm gonna spin you."

"Oh?" A look that was more challenge than doubt filled Sarah's eyes. "You have moves?"

Determined to prove himself, he put a little extra flair into twirling her about the dance floor. Her hand in his felt soft and especially feminine as he reeled her back into his arms.

"Oh, that was a surprise," she said, when her head once more rested on his shoulder.

Her body melded to his and, without a single hesitant step, they glided among the other couples. Unable to believe how well they fit together, he drew in a deep breath. The sweet, clean scent of roses and flowers picked fresh from the garden filled his nose. He leaned closer, searching for the source. For one brief moment, he let himself drink in the smell he'd always associate with Sarah and home. A smell he'd miss when he left here.

Suddenly, he didn't want to leave it all behind. Not his parents' house. His friends, new and old. Or Sarah, either.

When she tipped her head to his, it seemed like the most natural thing in the world to press his lips to hers. A heady mix of surprise and thankfulness filled him when she rose on tiptoe to kiss him back. For the long moment while they clung together, her heart beat in sync with his. Wishing that the moment could last forever, he pulled away just as the last few bars of the song came to a close. A camera flashed nearby while they lingered, their lips mere inches apart. Around them, people clapped. Bradley started.

*Oh man, what have I done?*

Drunk on a kiss that should never have taken place, he couldn't string two thoughts together. He stepped away from Sarah while he did his best to pretend that nothing had happened between them. But in spite of his efforts, something inside him argued that kissing Sarah was the smartest move he'd ever made. At the same time, shame heated the back of his neck. He was an engaged man, for goodness sake. He'd be a married one in a few days.

He turned to Sarah, intending to beg her forgiveness, to explain. But he had no words, because there was no explanation good enough to excuse what he'd done. What was he supposed to say—that he'd had no business taking her out on the dance floor, much less kissing her? That he'd given in to the heat of the moment?

Whatever he came up with, he wouldn't say he regretted it. Because he didn't. For as long as he lived, he'd judge every other kiss against that one, and he was pretty sure they'd all fall short. But he couldn't say that, either. Not here. Not now. The irony of being a Grammy-award-winning songwriter who couldn't find the right words struck home, and he groaned.

The last few bars of the slow dance ended. Her heart in her throat, Sarah stared up at Bradley. What had just happened? One minute, she and Bradley had been laughing and dancing. The next, they'd been kissing. And not just any old kiss. He'd kissed her like he meant it and, heaven help her, she'd kissed him right back. So, now what? Was this the moment when he'd sweep her into his arms, declare his love for her, and promise her forever?

Well, that was a foolish thought if she'd ever heard one. She dug it out by the roots and tossed it away, the same as she'd do for any weed that sprouted in her garden. She didn't love Bradley Suttons any more than he loved her. He was engaged to Catherine. Their kiss had been nothing more than a huge mistake. Wanting, needing to apologize before one moment of weakness ruined their friendship, she turned to face him.

"Evening, ya'll." Up on the stage, Sammy spoke into the microphone. "Now, we've got a very special treat for ya'll tonight. We have country superstar and Mill Town's own Bradley Suttons in the house."

Aware that every eye in the bar had zeroed in on them, Sarah edged a few steps out of the limelight. She'd bide her time. In a minute or two, Sammy would kick off the next number. Once everyone started dancing again, she and Bradley could talk about what had just happened and would never, ever, be repeated. Till then, she'd wait and pretend that everything was right as rain. While he waved to the crowd, she forced a fake smile to her lips and added her own applause to everyone else's.

"I'd like to invite him up to join the band for a

song." Sammy threw in a pleading look that no one in their right mind would refuse.

She sighed as, suddenly, a half-dozen fans mobbed Bradley. One of them gave him his hat. Another slipped a guitar into his hands. Surrounding him, they escorted him to the stage while she stood and…just watched.

"Howdy, ya'll." As if being called upon to perform with an unfamiliar instrument in a band he didn't know was something that happened to him every day of the week and twice on Sunday, Bradley leaned into the mic. "It's, uh, it's good to be home."

Sarah clasped her hands together. Tears stung her eyes when Bradley strummed the opening bars of "Love Don't Die Easy," the song that had won him a Grammy and catapulted him to the top of the charts. Was the song about them? Was it remotely possible that the feelings they'd shared as kids, the ones that had led them to promise to love and honor and, yes, even obey, still existed?

A voice at her elbow cut through the melody "What are you doing, Sarah?"

She struggled to compose herself. Hiding her emotions required more effort and time than she liked, but as soon as she could, she glanced up at Adam. "What are you talking about?"

"Come on. I've known you a long time." Other than her parents, no one knew her better. She and Adam had spent Sunday church services toddling around the nursery together. From first through twelfth grades, they'd attended the same schools, joined the same clubs. Their friendship had only strengthened once they'd both returned home after college. "You're falling in love with him, aren't you?"

She gave her head an emphatic shake. She didn't want to believe it. She couldn't love Bradley any more than he loved her. They were just two friends, helping out one another. "He's helping me on my ranch. I-I'm helping him plan his wedding."

"Exactly. *His* wedding." Adam's voice firmed. "He's marrying somebody else. He's leaving this town."

"I know that." Her voice shook. Even though he was leaving, even though she'd known that from the beginning, that didn't mean she had to like it.

"I care about you, Sarah." Compassion softened Adam's tone. "I just don't want to see you get hurt."

*I won't.*

How could she, if she didn't love Bradley? Oh, he was her friend. She cared for him. But love? No, that was foolish. So, he'd hugged her at the fishing hole yesterday. That didn't mean anything. Friends, hugged all the time. And yes, he'd kissed her, and she'd kissed him back, but that was a mistake, and as soon as she and Bradley had the chance to talk about it, they'd put it behind them and move on.

Other things weren't as easy to overlook, though. She let her thoughts drift. Her heart warmed whenever she stepped out onto her porch while the dew still sparkled on the grass and saw the lights shining in the window of his house. Each morning, her pulse leaped at the sight of Bradley as he cut across the field behind her house. They talked constantly while they worked on her fences. She'd told him practically everything about herself, from her deepest fears to her highest hopes, and he'd done the same.

She forced herself to look ahead, to the day after his wedding. Once he and Catherine left for their honeymoon, things around Mill Town would return to normal. She'd get that funding from the Equine Rehabilitation Fund in time to save her ranch and would go about her chores, same as usual. She'd have to make some small adjustments, of course. Instead of packing Bradley's ham-and-cheese sandwiches in her cooler each day, she'd make only one peanut butter and jelly sandwich for herself. It'd probably take her some time before she got used to pouring only one cup of coffee into the Thermos again. Without Bradley there to help her, it'd be a little harder to get the fences mended. She pictured herself going about her day, caring for the horses, feeding the goats, working in the garden…alone…and missing him every minute of every day.

Her breath hitched. Adam was right. She'd fallen in love with Bradley Suttons. She hadn't meant to do it. She hadn't even wanted to do it. But love had snuck up on her when she wasn't looking.

Adam was right about something else, too. Bradley was marrying someone else. A week from now, he'd be gone, out of her life forever. Her heart shattered at the thought.

She squeezed her eyes tight while the band played. How was she going to face Bradley? She couldn't look into his eyes and tell him their kiss had meant nothing to her. That would be a lie, and she'd promised she'd always tell him the truth. There might come a day when she'd have to break her word, but not today, not now, not over something as important as this.

Suddenly, she knew what she had to do. She had to leave. Now. She had some tough choices to make, and she couldn't make them here. Not in the middle of this crowd. Not with Bradley up on stage. She had to put some distance between them, needed time to think about what to do next.

Crossing to the bar where Adam sat, she grabbed her jacket and her purse. She ducked her head below the figures on the dance floor and, using the crowd for cover, she snuck out of the bar. On the sidewalk, she cast one last look behind her. Through the window, she saw Bradley in his element, singing his heart out in front of fans who loved him. His was a future that held no room for her. Certain she was making the right decision, she jumped in her truck and headed for home and a long, sleepless night.

# Chapter Twelve

Standing at the kitchen sink, Bradley sipped cold coffee while he stared out the window at the Standor ranch. Where was Sarah? Over the past couple of weeks, the two of them had fallen into a routine. While she fed the horses and farm animals first thing in the mornings, he'd sort through a few more of his parents' belongings or, if the mood was right, work on one of his new songs. Whenever he refilled his coffee cup, he'd catch little glimpses of her going about her chores and know that she wasn't ready for his help yet. But usually by the time the dew dried, she'd start gathering up the tools and equipment they'd need. That was when he'd join her, and they'd work late into the afternoon mending her fences.

But not today.

Today, when he really needed to talk to her, Sarah hadn't put in a single appearance. Not one of the horses had been turned out into the fields to graze. None of the three dogs that trailed her every step had raced through the front yard. Her truck hadn't moved from the spot where it'd been parked when Adam had driven him home last night.

She had to be avoiding him. That was the only explanation that made sense. Right now, she was probably standing at her own kitchen sink, drinking a cup of coffee while she shot dagger-filled looks his way. Not that he could blame her. Not after the stunt he'd pulled last night. But he could fix this. If she'd let him, he'd tell her how sorry he was for what he'd done and beg her to forgive him. The only problem was, the longer they went without clearing the air between them, the harder it'd be to go back to being friends again.

He glanced at the clock over the kitchen stove. Ten past nine. He'd give her another twenty minutes. Then, no matter what, he'd head for her place.

At the front door, someone rapped loudly. He swung toward it. "Sarah?" His pulse shifted into a hard, driving beat. "What happened to you last night?" he called on his way down the hall. "I waited—"

His footsteps slowed. Through the glass panes, he spotted the outline of a man. *Not Sarah*. His shoulders slumped. Propping one arm on the frame, he took a deep breath and opened the door.

"Morning!" Beneath the brim of a cream-colored Stetson that perfectly matched the color of his suit, the president of Mill Town Bank squinted.

"Mr. Fargo. I wasn't expecting you." Had he forgotten an appointment?

"Well, I came by to deliver some good news."

Without waiting for an invitation, James stepped across the threshold. "We got a solid offer on your house. They want to move in right away. It's an all-cash offer..."

Much as he didn't want to throw a wet blanket over James's enthusiasm, he needed to stop the banker. Bradley shook his head. Two weeks ago, he'd have been thrilled to get the house off his hands. Even a week ago, he might have jumped at the chance to sell. But things had changed. "I'm not sure I want to sell. I was thinking I might just keep the house."

The lost commission sent disappointment flickering across James Fargo's face, but the bank president was a consummate professional. It took less than a beat for him to realize the benefits of having a superstar in Mill Town's back yard. He smiled broadly. "Well, that's good news."

"I'm beginning to see how important it is for you to hold onto your roots."

"Maybe you can talk some sense into your neighbor." James aimed a finger toward Sarah's house. "She's gonna lose her ranch soon if she doesn't figure out a way to pay her mortgage."

Bradley frowned. Sarah? Lose her ranch? That didn't make any sense. "What do you mean?"

"Well, she's waiting for some funding to come in, but she's way behind on her payments." James nodded to himself as he spoke. "People leave her their sick or old horses to take care of. They don't pay their bills, and she gets stuck."

"Huh." Of course, Sarah would never consider any alternative, other than continuing to feed and care for them. Her love for animals was one of the things that drew him to her.

"And, uh, her flower business isn't enough to carry the ranch."

"Is that right." Why was this the first he was hearing about all this? He'd been in town now for two weeks, and in all that time, Sarah had never once mentioned a looming financial crisis. And here he'd thought they were friends. Good friends. For one crazy second last night, he'd thought they were even more than that. But he'd been wrong. They weren't friends at all. Because a true friend would never let the bank take her ranch without at least mentioning her problems to the man she'd once married, the one who had the resources to help her out of her jam. Disappointed by the revelation, he turned away from the door and pressed a hand over the empty spot in his heart.

Sarah kneeled among the flowers in the shade of the big maple tree. Her movements stilted and slow after barely sleeping a wink all night, she snipped the stem of a white rose and trimmed the sharp thorns with a pair of sheers. She laid the finished blossom in her gathering basket.

"Twenty-two," she whispered. Or was it twenty-three? She'd lost track again and, with an exasperated sigh, counted the long stems for the third time since she'd started. Normally, working with the roses restored her soul and salved her spirit. Today, though, all she saw were the thorns among the flowers. The velvety softness of the petals grated on her skin like fine sandpaper. She longed to escape the cloying sweetness of the blossoms.

Soon, she told herself. As soon as she filled the order for two dozen, she'd deliver them to the florist in town. Then, she'd take one of the horses out for a long, solitary ride. The feel of wind whipping through her hair, the sound of hooves hammering the ground beneath her, the gelding's powerful muscles bunching and extending as they raced across the open field— surely, that ought to make her feel better.

Sadly, she tsked. It'd take more than a horseback ride to cure what ailed her. After her chat with Adam last night, she'd had a long, heart-to-heart with herself. She didn't much like what she'd learned. During her senior year in veterinary school, she'd sworn she'd never, ever get involved with a man who couldn't be faithful to her alone. Not again. And yet, that was exactly what she'd done. She didn't know when or how, but she had to admit it. She'd fallen head over heels for a man who was engaged to someone else. Which left her no choice. She had to make a clean break with Bradley before things went even one step farther.

"Mornin'."

Her traitorous heart shifted into high gear at the sound of the familiar voice of the very person she'd vowed to avoid. Sarah froze. Determined to make the smart move, to act on her decision, she refused to let herself so much as glance in Bradley's direction. Instead, she tossed a vague, "Hey," over one shoulder while she clung to the next flower stem as if her life depended on the precise way she snipped its thorns.

"Last night was fun."

Not really. Not when the press of his lips against hers led to a sleepless night. She shrugged.

"I tried to find you when I was leaving but…"

Apparently, Bradley wasn't going to take her cold shoulder for a hint. She supposed she'd have to answer him. "Oh, yeah. Sorry. I had to duck out. I was exhausted, and—and I got so much work to get done."

"Well, I'll go get my tools and get to work on the fences."

She heard the rustle of Bradley's boots through the grass and knew he'd drop everything to help her out. But that was part of the problem, wasn't it? Though they'd started out with the best of intentions, they'd gotten too close. Now, there was nothing left for her to do but shut the door. "No, you take the day off," she called while she snipped another blossom.

Bradley moved closer. "Is everything okay?"

She heard the hurt in his voice. Heaven help her, she wanted to run to him, to put her arms around him and tell him everything was fine between them. But it wouldn't be the truth. Not now that she'd fallen for him. She forced a steadiness she didn't feel into her voice. "Everything's fine. I just—I gotta get this done."

*Why can't he take the hint and just leave?*

Instead of heading back to his own house, to a life that would never include her, to the woman he'd promised to marry, Bradley hopped over a row of mature blossoms and stepped closer. "Yeah. I wanted to thank you for looking after my yard and my flowers all these years."

She rocked back on her heels. No matter what happened between them in the future, Bradley deserved to know that she'd always hold onto her warm feelings for his family. "That's not a problem. You and your family were great neighbors to us."

"Well, I—I wanted to pay you for the work that you did. I feel like it's only fair—"

"No, no." She should have known the president of Mill Town Bank was up to no good when she'd spotted his car parked in Bradley's driveway this morning. She pressed her fingers into the dirt. James had no right discussing her personal finances with anyone. Much less her neighbor. Why, she had half a mind to grab her keys, head into town, and give the banker an earful. Maybe she would, too. As soon as she dealt with the mess he'd made of things. Though, if James had just kept his mouth shut for a little while longer, she wouldn't have to deal with this at all. In a matter of days, Bradley and Catherine would have their wedding and jet off on their honeymoon. And that could have been that. Once they returned to their own lives, she doubted Bradley would ever give her a second thought. But now...

"I know what you're up to. You been talking to James Fargo?"

When she swung to study Bradley's face, the guilt in his eyes told her she was on the right track, and James had been talking out of school. She squeezed a handful of soil between her fingers. She could have gone to Bradley weeks ago, asked him for a loan she might never be able to repay. But she'd had too much pride to take advantage of their friendship. Weren't the gossip rags chock full of stories of movie stars and professional athletes whose friends and families sponged off them? She'd never wanted to be lumped in with those people. Now that Bradley suspected the worst, though, he'd probably insist on bailing her out. That left her with just one option. She'd have to do the one thing she'd sworn she'd never do—she'd have to lie to him. James had left her no choice. She swallowed the bitter pill and took a breath. "You don't have to worry about me. I got my letter, and my funding came through. So, I'm going to be just fine."

Later, she couldn't remember the rest of the conversation. She imagined they'd exchanged the usual pleasantries before Bradley headed back the way he'd come. Whatever they'd said, the blurred image of Bradley's retreating figure through her tears was the only thing she recalled.

Catherine shuffled the stack of cards that had arrived in response to her wedding invitations. So far, not a single important figure in the movie industry had sent their regrets. She pursed her lips. With so many people willing to fly to Italy to see her walk down the aisle, she'd have to make a few adjustments. She scanned the elaborate chart that had been custom-designed to display seating for three hundred guests. The pearlescent tips of her fingernails flashed as she shifted Bradley's manager to a table a little farther away from the dais in order to make room for the reporter from *People Magazine*. There. She smiled. No one would ever know about the seating change.

"Hello!" Dressed to the nines as always, Margaret strode into the room. She marched straight across the open space, stopping just shy of the coffee table. Like a general inspecting her troops, she studied the seating chart. "So, are you still planning on going to Texas this weekend?"

"I am." Catherine gave her agent a smile she didn't have to force. Between her work on the set and all the details of organizing a destination wedding, she hadn't had a spare moment to miss Bradley while he'd been gone. Now that she'd wrapped up her part in the movie though, it surprised her that she missed his company as much as she did. She'd decided to take a day or two to decompress, spend another one at the spa, then head south by the end of the week. "I'm actually really excited to see where Bradley came from."

"Oh. Hmmm." Paper rustled as Margaret revealed something from behind her back. Skirting the coffee table, she slid onto the couch. "Someone sent me this early this morning."

The folded newspaper that slapped precisely into Catherine's hands sent a rush of nervous energy through her. She opened the paper to the front page where a bold headline announced, *Country Star Comes Home To Wed*.

A picture of Bradley on the stage of some no-name bar filled most of the space above the fold. She barely glanced at it. Her attention narrowed in on a second, smaller photograph. This one showed her fiancé standing unacceptably close to a very attractive woman. Her heart sank.

"Who is this?" Catherine tapped the brunette's image.

"According to the article, Sarah Standor. A childhood friend." Margaret's pursed lips tightened in distaste.

"The girl who sent the letter and the ring." Her fingers tensed with the urge to gouge the other woman's eyes out. "The nerdy girl with braids?"

"Hmmm. She aged well." Margaret leaned in. "You need to go to Texas. Now."

Catherine's breath stalled in her chest. If the love-struck expression on Bradley's face was any indication, she didn't need Margaret to tell her there was no time to waste. Forget seating charts, towering wedding cakes, and hand-stitched twenty-thousand-dollar gowns. If she didn't get to Texas—and soon—there'd be no wedding.

Catherine snapped her fingers. "Call my travel

agent. Book me on the next flight. Tell my assistant to start packing." She slapped the offensive newspaper onto the seating chart. The carefully arranged name tags scattered. Springing to her feet, she marched to her closet, where she began yanking clothes from their hangers. And all the while, she wondered why Bradley had never looked at her with such adoring eyes.

# Chapter Thirteen

Sarah set the heavy feed pails on the barn's straw-covered floor. Unlatching the first stall, she mopped her brow on the sleeve of her shirt and whispered a mild oath. Time dragged without Bradley at her side, without his stories and laughter to brighten the hours. The chores she'd sailed through these past few weeks when she looked forward to spending the rest of the day with him, now sapped her energy. Well, that was what she got for letting her guard down, for daring to hope for something more than friendship between them. But no more. From here on out, she'd face whatever challenges life threw at her on her own.

"Hey."

The unexpected sound of Bradley's voice stopped her in her tracks. "Hey," she echoed without putting a drop of enthusiasm into it.

His booted feet scuffed down the aisle between the stalls. "Are you avoiding me?" He drew nearer.

"No." No more than she'd avoid the bubonic plague. "I've just been real busy." As if to prove her point, she dumped one of the buckets of oats and beet pulp into a trough.

"Fences look good."

Much to her dismay, while she stacked the empty feed pails, Bradley propped one arm on the gate to a stall and leaned on it as if he intended to stay a while. She shoved a hank of hair behind one ear. Pushing her way past the tall figure who nearly blocked her path, she murmured, "I gotta get going. I got a flower delivery."

"Well, I'll come with you." Bradley lingered behind her.

"No, I got it." She shoved an extra measure of sharpness into her tone. She was acting like a jerk, but the last thing she needed was to get trapped in her truck with Bradley beside her all the way into town. She yanked her hands free of their work gloves. She'd nearly reached the exit—and escape—when he spoke again.

"I decided to keep the house," he announced. "I'm not selling it."

The news got her attention. Her measured footsteps slowed. She pivoted. "Why?" *Because of me?* Her heart thudded.

"It's home." Bradley shrugged. "I think you helped me remember that."

So, he planned on sticking around, did he? Clearly, he hadn't thought this through. She folded her arms across her chest. "Do you think Catherine will like it here?"

"Well, I don't see why not." Bradley's pointed glance took in the goats in their pen, the hens' nests in one corner. "It's beautiful and calm. People are friendly. The air is clean."

The man was delusional. Catherine Mann lived in a 9,000-square-foot mansion in Bel-Air. She owned a four-bedroom condo on the Upper East Side of Manhattan. Her idea of "roughing it" was a $2,000-a-night stay in a ritzy spa without room service. Someone like that was *not* going to take one look at Mill Town, with its lone diner and few shops, and instantly decide she wanted to spend the rest of her life here. Sarah shook her head. Bradley was in for a rude awakening, but it wasn't her place to point it out. She marched toward her truck.

"Hey!" Angry footsteps pounded the ground behind her. "What's going on with you?" he demanded.

Sarah froze. This was the moment when she should blame her bad mood on the weather, or maybe stress. She should laugh and tell him not to worry about it, that things would be all right between them in a day or two. The trouble was, she'd be lying. She'd fallen for Bradley and, while she knew deep down in her bones that they had no future together, she still cared for him. They were still friends. As such, didn't she owe it to him to at least warn him that he was about to make the biggest mistake of his life?

Summoning her courage, she spun to face him. "You want the truth? 'Cause like you said, you got a lotta people in your life who tell you what they think you want to hear. So maybe you like it that way."

Bradley propped both hands at his waist. His jaw firmed. His slow, "I'd rather hear the truth," sounded like it came from his heart.

"Okay." She took a breath. "Well, you're about to marry a woman you barely know." When Bradley reeled back a step, she forced herself to overlook the motion, to tell him what he needed to hear. "You don't know her favorite color. You don't know her favorite flower. You don't even know if she wants to have a family." Her voice caught, but she refused to let it slow her down. Now that she'd started, she had to finish. "I mean, it seems to me you know nothing about her at all."

Bradley's brows slammed together. "No. I know everything I need to know," he insisted.

She wished that was true, but the man was just lying to himself. Every bride enjoyed planning her special day. Someone like Catherine, someone used to standing in the spotlight, would bask in having the focus solely on her. So, why wasn't she here? Sarah stared down at the ground and swallowed. Crying would only muddy the waters.

"Why are you here planning your wedding without her? Why am I here making all the decisions she should be making?" Tears clogged her throat. She fought them down. Raising her head, she stared straight into Bradley's dark-brown eyes. If she was going to make him see the truth, she had to be strong. "*Where* is she?"

"I told you. She's—she's busy filming."

*Not so.* According to the latest gossip magazines, shooting on Catherine's next blockbuster movie had wrapped up over a week ago. Yet Bradley's bride-to-be had yet to put in an appearance.

When Bradley folded his arms in as defensive a gesture as she'd ever seen, she mopped her face with one hand. He might deny it, but somewhere deep inside, he knew she was telling the truth. "Okay, look." She expelled a heated breath. "You and I have been friends a long time. So, I'm gonna shoot you straight."

Bradley glanced at her sideways. "All right."

"Okay." *Lord, give me strength.* She had to get this right. "You can't marry Catherine Mann. You don't love her." Her voice broke.

Bradley closed the distance between them. "I do. I do…love her."

His slight hesitation told her he was losing his grip on the lie he'd been telling himself for the past few months. It was time to present her final piece of evidence.

"Why did you kiss me?" she asked. She'd always believed Bradley was too good a man, too honorable to cheat on the woman he loved. But he'd kissed her while he was engaged to Catherine. Which meant he either wasn't the man she'd thought he was, or he didn't love the woman who wore his ring. Praying she was right about him, she searched his face for answers.

"I shouldn't have done that." Misery moved into Bradley's eyes and set up shop. "All right, I'm sorry."

He shook his head. "I just—I just got caught up in the music and the…and the moment."

"So that's all that was? You got" —she sneered— "caught up in the moment."

"Yeah."

She dried her tears with the backs of her hands. Did he make a habit of kissing other women whenever the moment was right? She didn't want to believe that he'd lie and cheat, that he thought that kind of behavior was acceptable. He was better than that, wasn't he? She studied his firmly set jaw, peered into the eyes that refused to meet her own. Maybe he was afraid. The year he'd turned thirteen, he'd lost the two people he'd loved the most in the world. Something like that had to have left scars.

"Look. I get that you're scared." She sighed. "Okay. You got your heart broken as a kid. And you are afraid to love too much, ever again."

"Nah." Bradley gave his head an emphatic shake. Without saying another word, he walked away from her.

His denial only reinforced her certainty that she was on the right track. Refusing to let him go until she'd said her piece, she dogged his footsteps. "Well, you know what? Love is scary! It's terrifying to put your heart out there." She should know. She was shaking in her boots right now.

"But you do it anyway. You do it in spite of the fear. Because a life without love, that's just half a life. And you don't get married 'cause you like the same things.

And 'cause you live similar lifestyles." Unable to stop them, she scrubbed at the tears that streamed down her cheeks. "You get married 'cause you can't stand the thought of not being together. You get married 'cause you love the other person. With your whole heart."

*Like I love you.*

Disbelief marched across Bradley's face. "That's just—that's just a fantasy."

"Maybe it is," she admitted. Her energy spent, she softened. "But I don't think you should settle for less."

In her dreams, this was the moment when Bradley came to his senses. When he realized he didn't love Catherine Mann. When he knew beyond a shadow of a doubt that *she* was the woman he loved. This was the part where he'd sweep her off her feet and promise that, no matter what the future had in store for them, they'd face it together. Forever.

But this wasn't a dream. And Bradley, apparently, was no knight in shining armor. The man country music fans all but worshipped shoved his hands into the back pockets of his jeans. His expression hardening, he leaned forward until mere inches separated his face from hers. "You know, just 'cause you knew me when I was a kid, it doesn't mean you know me now."

What little fight Sarah had left in her rode out on a long exhale. Shame on her. She had no one to blame but herself for seriously misjudging Bradley. Empty inside, she wiped her eyes. "Yeah. I guess you're right." It was time to end this. "Look. You and me had a deal, okay. You'd help me mend my fences" —she nodded to the sturdy fencing that surrounded the ranch— "and I'd help you plan your wedding." Her voice caught. "So…" Aware that she was seconds away from breaking down completely, she hurried to get the words out. "I guess we're done."

She spun toward her truck. She might as well admit it—she'd been wrong about Bradley all along. Though he didn't love Catherine Mann, he'd gotten himself engaged to marry her. And even after she'd shown him all the reasons why going forward with the wedding was the wrong thing to do, he was determined to see it through. Well, she'd done all she could do to change his mind.

Not really caring where they landed, she tossed her work gloves among the flowers in the bed of her truck. Emotionally wrung out, she jerked the driver's door open, slid behind the wheel and, wanting, needing to put as much distance between them as possible, drove away.

In the rearview mirror, Bradley stood in the middle of the driveway and stared after her. She wrenched her gaze forward. The kiss they'd shared meant nothing. Bradley Suttons wasn't her Mr. Forever. He wasn't even close.

# Chapter Fourteen

"**T**his is me. Who are you?"

Sitting on the edge of his bed, Bradley plowed his fingers through his hair. Not so long ago, he'd thought Catherine's voicemail message was every bit as cute as his bride-to-be. Not anymore. Not when she let his calls go to voicemail far more often than she picked up. Wasn't he every bit as important as whatever she happened to be doing at the moment?

"Hey, Catherine. It's me," he said at the beep. After a sleepless night and an equally restless day, he wished his was the one phone call she always rushed to answer. Or that she wanted to spend time with him more than she wanted to do anything else in the world. But that wasn't the kind of relationship they'd signed on for, and they both knew it. "Call me when you get this?" he finished. "We need to talk."

A knock on the door downstairs made his stomach clench. "Sarah?" His heart pounded.

Instantly on his feet, he hustled toward the stairs. It was about time Sarah showed up. He hadn't seen hide nor hair of the girl next door since their talk yesterday, though it wasn't for lack of trying. He'd scoured the barn looking for her, but she must have gotten an early start because, by the time he'd shown up at sunrise, every stall had been mucked and the horses put out to pasture. When she hadn't been in the garden, he'd returned to his house, where he'd stared out the window at her ranch for another full hour, hoping to catch sight of her. But she, like Catherine, was nowhere to be found.

Cutting through the living room that boasted a comfortable, lived-in look thanks to the countless hours he'd spent unpacking and cleaning, he practiced what he'd say when he answered the door.

First off, he owed Sarah a huge apology. He'd had no right to treat her the way he had. She'd meant well, even if they'd never be on the same page as far as marriage and relationships went. She was the closest thing he had to family in this part of the country. Like all relatives, they'd have their disagreements, but they'd always be friends. Best friends. That would never change. No matter what happened between them, he wanted her at his wedding. She had to be there. Eager to convince her, he pulled the door wide.

But it wasn't Sarah who stood on his porch. It was Catherine. His mouth gaped open. He closed it. Opened it again. "Catherine! You're here!"

"Uh-huh." An instant later, his arms filled with her soft curves. The signature cologne that reeked of money and prestige filled his nose as Catherine pressed the length of her body against his. Bouncy curls that didn't feel nearly as soft as they looked brushed his shoulders when she nestled against his neck. "We're getting married in a couple of days," she murmured in a breathy on-screen voice. "I thought it was time I reclaimed my cowboy." Cupping her elegantly manicured fingers around his cheeks, she lingered a bit too long over a welcoming kiss.

Bradley firmly set her at arm's length. "Let me get your bags." Confusion swirled in his head while he dashed onto the porch. Wheeling her small suitcase and overnight case into the room a second later, he fought a sudden nervousness while his bride-to-be surveyed the house he'd worked so hard to bring back to life.

"I thought you were selling this place." Catherine cast a wary glance at the floor as if she half expected to spot a cow patty in the living room. Careful lest the white designer frock she wore brush against any of the furniture, she paced the middle of the room. "Wasn't that the whole point of coming here?"

"Well, I—I was." Bradley tucked her luggage into one corner. "Then I got here and realized, maybe, I should hold onto it." He skimmed his fingers over his dad's old recliner.

"Why?"

"Well, I grew up here. This is my home." He fought to overlook the condescension in Catherine's tone. She didn't know that his mom had sewn the curtains on the windows. That his father had carved the mantle out of solid maple. Or that every piece of furniture, every picture on the wall held a special place in his heart. He moved toward his bride-to-be. "Listen, I'm so glad you're here. I learned so much about myself over the last couple of weeks."

They had a lot to discuss. He'd tell her all about the songs he'd written. About his new skill at horseback riding. About the fish he'd caught down at the fishing hole. She'd fill him in on everything she'd been doing while they were apart.

Catherine traced one long, red nail through the air in a circle centered on his chest. "What are you wearing?"

He glanced down at the pair of well-worn jeans and denim shirt he'd pulled from one of the trunks upstairs. "Just some old clothes. Work clothes."

"Work?" Catherine sniffed.

What did she think he was supposed to do—hire an army of strangers to unpack his parents' belongings, tend to his mother's roses, mend Sarah's fences? He took a breath. "Look. I thought we could keep this house. As a home base. For when we're not working. Then, we could spend time here with our children. Teach them how to fish and ride horses. Give 'em something real. Something out of the spotlight."

"Our—our children?" Catherine's nervous laughter sent a shiver down his spine.

"You want to have children, don't you?" Despite his best efforts, he frowned. "I mean, I—I know we never discussed it, but..."

Catherine gave her head a dismissive shake. "We love each other, and we're getting married." The tips of her nails dug into his skin when she placed the palm of one hand on his chest. "We have a lifetime to learn everything we need to know about each other." Cupping his chin again, she pressed in to brush his lips with a tender kiss. "I want what you want."

He fought to keep his balance. Catherine's response hadn't told him a thing. Did she mean she wanted the house...or the children...or the whole package? Before he had a chance to ask, she pushed away from him. As if she couldn't wait to go someplace else, be someplace else, she flounced toward the stairs. "So, why don't I get changed. And you can make reservations someplace nice. And we can go out on the town and celebrate."

Feeling a little like he was playing a role in one of her movies, Bradley stuck his hands in his pockets. Barely five minutes had passed since Catherine had breezed back into his life, and they'd already hit a snag. "Well, there's a diner in town, but there aren't any fancy restaurants close by."

Catherine's eyebrows dipped low. "Where do people eat?"

He laughed. Only someone who'd been born with the proverbial silver spoon in their mouth would ever ask such a question, but he'd answer it. "At home. They cook."

Catherine's eyes widened. Her jaw unhinged. Seeing the concerned look that bordered on fear on her face, Bradley took pity on her. She was his fiancée, after all. She couldn't help it if her idea of a home-cooked meal was take-out from a five-star restaurant. She'd never known any other kind of life. He cupped her shoulders in his hands. "It's going to be great," he promised. "Okay? We're gonna get up early tomorrow morning. I'm gonna take you on that hike. Then, we can go fishing. You're going to love it. I promise."

The tiniest bit of skepticism faded from Catherine's eyes. She gave her head a gentle shake that didn't disturb her carefully coifed hair. "As long as we're together, everything's perfect."

Moments later, Bradley placed Catherine's luggage in the guest room. As he laid out fresh towels for his soon-to-be-bride, he paused. Catherine had said all the right things, offered all the right assurances. Why then, had he heard a false note in her voice? Why didn't her actions, her emotions, ring true?

He shrugged. After this much time apart, they both probably had a case of pre-wedding jitters and were trying too hard. Things would smooth out between them once they'd had a chance to spend more time together. At least, he hoped they would.

"Have you, uh, seen your neighbor?" In a series of dainty steps, Catherine eased down the muddy incline to the beach where fist-sized rocks covered the ground. "The one who sent you the ring?"

"Sarah?" Toting an ice chest, the tackle box, and two fishing rods, plus a backpack filled with what

Catherine had termed "essentials," Bradley waited for his fiancée to catch up. "Yeah, she has a horse rescue ranch next door." He lifted their two fishing poles in the direction of the neighboring property.

"Wonderful." Catherine's focus on her shoes, she slowly picked her way across the rocks.

"She depends on funding to keep it running. I'm not sure she got it." Though Sarah had insisted that her grant had come through, he wasn't sure he believed her. "I offered to help, but she's too stubborn to let me."

In a tone that said she probably wouldn't be half as generous, Catherine murmured, "You're such a good man."

"The bank's threatening to sell the ranch if she doesn't come up with the money soon."

"What a shame."

"She's a great girl. She helped us plan our whole wedding." He hoped Sarah and Catherine would get along, especially since they'd be neighbors soon. Despite the fight they'd had the last time he'd seen her, he still considered Sarah his best friend.

A bleating noise rose over the sound of babbling water, the rustle of wind in the trees, the bird calls. He glanced over one shoulder at Catherine. His fiancée had stopped to chat with someone on the cell phone she carried with her wherever she went. The one she rarely answered when he called. He ground his back teeth together. "Hello!"

Feeling a little like an intruder, he listened as she

gave the caller directions to the ranch. "What was that all about?" he asked when she slipped the phone back into her pocket.

"I just ordered a few things to make our wedding a little more comfortable." Catherine's voice dropped to a whisper while, hips swaying, she moved toward him.

"I told you, I took care of it." For two weeks straight, he and Sarah had spent every spare minute planning the special day. They'd covered every possible detail. "I ordered a cake. And flowers. And—"

"And I'm sure you did a great job," Catherine said, making it sound as if nothing he and Sarah had done could possibly live up to her standards. "But we'll have our rehearsal dinner and our sweet, little barn wedding. And then we'll get to Italy and" —she sighed—"back to our real lives."

Her tone set his teeth on edge, and he stiffened. He and Sarah had worked hard, very hard, to plan the perfect wedding for Catherine. To have her downplay their efforts, well, it just wasn't right. But then again, nothing else about his fiancée's trip had gone according to plan. He thought they'd agreed on an early morning fishing trip but, claiming the hamburgers he'd fried for their supper last night had left her nauseated, his bride-to-be had slept in this morning. When she finally had gotten out of bed, she'd screamed bloody murder after her hour-long shower had drained the hot water tank. Her insistence on spending another hour in front of the mirror before she'd declared herself ready to step onto the porch had tested his patience. He'd nearly lost it completely when she'd taken one look at the horses he'd saddled and had quietly announced that she didn't know how to ride. Apparently, a stunt double handled all the horseback scenes in her movies. Who knew? Certainly not him. He'd never been invited to visit one of her movie sets. When they'd finally headed for the creek on foot, Catherine hadn't complained. Not exactly. But she had pointed out that her Valentino ballet flats weren't up to the rigors of walking through fields and over rocks.

He'd been seriously tempted to ask why she hadn't packed a pair of boots when she'd known all along he planned to take her hiking and fishing. But they'd both been on edge this morning, and the odds were that Catherine would take the question as criticism, something she didn't deal well with. Rather than running the risk of ruining their day altogether, he'd opted for the high road.

Catherine hadn't grown up on a ranch. Maybe she hadn't realized how a walk through the forest differed from a walk in the park. She certainly had no idea how much work he and Sarah had put into cleaning the barn or seeing to the hundred-and-one other details for the wedding. He gave himself a stern reminder that his bride was probably feeling out of place and uncertain. Hadn't he felt the same way the first time he'd stepped on stage in Nashville? The first time he'd been interviewed on live television? Catherine had helped him past those milestones. Now it was his turn to return the favor.

"All right." He straightened his hat. If she wanted to add a few fancy touches to make herself feel more at home during the ceremony, he'd go along with that.

Standing in the middle of the river a short while later, Bradley cast his line clear to the other bank. As his lure drifted down stream, he glanced at Catherine. Had he been wrong to overrule her pleas to stay on dry ground? He shook his head. Wading into the water was half the fun of fishing. Certain she'd enjoy the sport if she gave it half a chance, he'd helped her don a pair of waders. He'd held her hand while she'd navigated the slippery, moss-covered river bed. He'd covered all the basics, even thrown out her line for her. Not that it had done any good. She hadn't made a single cast, hadn't once jiggled her lure. How was she going to catch a fish if she didn't even try? He crossed his fingers. Catherine might look bored now, but wait until she felt the first tug on her line, landed her first fish. He and Sarah had laughed and jumped around like a pair of kids the day he'd caught that big trout. He wanted to share that same experience with his fiancée.

"You know, I love this place," he told her while he made another long cast.

"I can see that. So..." Despite his warnings to watch her step, she hobbled across the slippery rocks toward him. "How long do we actually need to stay out here for?"

He reeled in a good section of his line. "You'll

know when you're done." Hopefully, not before she at least got a bite.

"Okay. I'm done."

Bradley swallowed a sigh. Well, that hadn't taken long. They'd hardly been here fifteen minutes. Reluctantly, he began reeling in so he could help Catherine back across the rocks. Before he could, she spun toward the shore. As if the rules about being careful didn't applied to her, she sloshed through the water.

"Wait!" he called. Even with her waders, the footing was treacherous.

He might as well have saved his breath. Catherine didn't stop. She didn't slow down.

Bradley braced for the inevitable. Sure enough, not two seconds later, Catherine lost her footing. Loosing a scream shrill enough to startle the birds from the trees, she fell face-first into the water. Before he could react, or even help her remember to simply stand up in the shallow water, the fast-moving current pulled her farther away from him.

"Catherine!" He tried to get her attention, but it was no use. Realizing she'd never hear him over the sound of her own screams, he tossed his fishing rod aside and dove in after her. The hard work he'd put into building fences with Sarah paid off when, his arms churning, he reached his bride-to-be in a matter of seconds. While she screeched at him to "Get me out of here!" he made quick work of getting her to shore.

"Sit down here." He helped her onto a chair-sized

boulder and took a breath. Catherine had been lucky. She could have hit her head on the rocks or gotten all scraped up, but she looked and sounded okay. A little waterlogged, perhaps, and madder than a wet hen about it, but as soon as she realized she'd walk away unscathed, she'd probably laugh about the whole episode.

"I can't believe you made me do that," Catherine sputtered without showing the slightest trace of humor.

*Wait a minute.* It hadn't been his idea to go rushing around on the slippery rocks. Hadn't he warned her to be careful?

He clenched his teeth. "Let me get these off of you," he said, grasping one wader by the heel.

Catherine shuddered when water poured out of the upended boot. "Oh, disgusting!" she declared. "I am never, ever doing this again."

And, by the determined look in her eyes, Bradley knew she meant it. He sighed again. So much for his hope that the incident would get etched in their memories as one of those funny stories married couples told. Or that, years from now, when friends visited them at the ranch, she'd turn to him with laughter in her eyes and ask, "Remember the day when I fell in the river?"

# Chapter Fifteen

"Well, the postman delivered a bumper crop of mail today. Didn't he, Cooper?"

Beside her, the cocker spaniel's tail beat against the chenille spread. Sitting cross-legged on her bed, Sarah poked through the stacks of bills and advertisements. Her heart rate sped up as she eyed the yellow second notices that glowed through most of the cellophane windows. A few bright red final notices added more color to the stack, and her pulse quickened again. She groaned.

Which one should she open first? Did it matter? She didn't have enough money to pay the bills. Her last floral delivery hadn't even covered her order at the feed store, but what was she supposed to do—let the horses in her care starve? That wasn't the answer. It couldn't be. So, she'd done the only thing she could under the circumstances: she'd maxed out her last remaining credit card to buy enough oats and beet pulp to get them through the first week in June.

She stirred a finger through the pile. As she

did, a slim, white envelope slid out from under an advertisement for horse shampoo and conditioner. She snatched the envelope from the stack. Why hadn't she seen it before? Her head throbbed in time with her heartbeat as she read Equine Rehabilitation Fund in the return address. This was it. The answer to all her prayers.

"Cooper." She held the important notice in front of the aged spaniel. "We got it."

Her hands shaking, she slid one finger under the flap. Had the Equine Fund approved her entire request? Would there be enough to bring her mortgage up to date? To cover all her bills? Her breath stalled as she withdrew the single page and flipped it open.

*We regret to inform you…*

"Oh, no," she whispered. The world spun. Pain rippled through her chest. Beside her, Cooper whimpered. Tears welled in her eyes as she lifted the older dog into her arms.

There was no hope, no putting off the inevitable. Later this week, she'd be forced to walk into James Fargo's office and hand over the deed to the ranch. What would happen to her horses then? Where would she and her dogs go? What was to become of them?

In her arms, Cooper whined. Sarah pressed the dog closer, but the soothing reassurances she wanted to give him wouldn't come.

It wasn't fair. But then, so little had been lately. Was it fair that she and Bradley had reconnected after so many years apart, only to have their friendship—

and any hope of something more, something deeper—crash and burn? Was it right for him to marry a woman he barely knew? Or for her to be left with this aching hole in her center?

Years had passed since her last serious relationship. After all that time, she'd nearly given up on finding the forever kind of love her parents had shared. Instead, she'd poured her heart and soul into providing a safe and secure environment for abused animals. But then, Bradley had come back to Mill Town, and for one brief moment, she'd dared to dream of forever. When that hope had died, it had driven a knife straight into her heart. The letter rejecting her grant request from the Equine Rehabilitation Fund had finished the job of shattering her. She'd lost…everything.

She sprawled on the bed, clutched the dog close, and sobbed.

Catherine slipped the items she needed into the oversized Hermes purse and peered out the window toward the neighboring ranch. Spotting Sarah near the barn, she smiled tightly. Bradley had been quite secretive about the errand he needed to run this morning, but it didn't take a genius to figure out that he'd driven into town to pick up a wedding gift for her. He'd probably chosen something sweet and sentimental. A trinket she would tuck away in a special spot along with pictures of their quaint wedding in a barn. But for now, she was glad he had something to occupy his time. His absence gave her just the opportunity she'd been hoping for, and she set out, determined to have a heart-to-heart with the girl next door.

"We're gonna get you better in no time." The short brunette ran one hand over the mane of a quarter horse that, even to Catherine's inexperienced eyes, had seen better days.

So, this was the infamous Sarah, was it? The one whose name popped up in every conversation she'd had with Bradley in the two, long, miserable days she'd spent in Mill Town? Catherine eyed the woman closely. What did her fiancé see in her?

Sarah had a sort of earthy charm, she supposed, watching as the woman doused the horse's side with medicine and tended to a nasty-looking wound. But, from where she stood, it didn't appear that Bradley's neighbor put much effort into her appearance, not if the broken-down boots, the well-worn jeans, and unfashionable chambray shirt were her normal attire. She didn't spend much time in front of the mirror, either, judging from the lack of makeup on her pale cheeks. Not so much as a single stroke of eye shadow glistened from beneath her brows. She eyed Sarah's puffy eyes and the flyaway ends that escaped a haphazard ponytail. A couple of cold cucumber slices and fifteen minutes on the chaise lounge would work wonders, as would an appointment with a good stylist.

Not that she'd suggest either. After all, why give the competition any pointers? Whether she knew it or not, Sarah had already wormed her way into

Bradley's heart. But she wouldn't stay there long, not if Catherine had anything to say about it.

She skimmed one hand over tailored white jeans that fit like a second skin. Smoothing the hem of a sleeveless blouse that went perfectly with her three-inch heels and designer bag, she halted well short of the mud and muck that surrounded Sarah. "Good morning," she called, raising her voice above the sounds of chickens squawking and goats bleating.

"Catherine! Hi! So nice to meet you." Sarah's eyes widened. Her face turned a lovely shade of star-struck pink. The tools and supplies she'd been using fell to the ground. Her color deepened as she closed the distance between them while she tugged at a pair of rubber gloves. "I'm a huge fan." She extended a hand.

Catherine arched one eyebrow.

"Oh!" Sarah jerked her still-gloved fingers out of reach. "Sorry!"

"Thanks." Catherine folded her own hands at her waist. A good part of her plan relied on catching their neighbor off-guard. So far, so good. She mustered her friendliest smile for her fiancé's childhood friend. "Bradley told me what you're doing here. Rescuing horses. I'm—" she did her best not to wrinkle her nose, "—very impressed."

Sarah balled the glove and stuck it in a back pocket. "I love the work."

"It's beautiful here. I can see why Bradley likes it so much." He actually enjoyed hiking and fishing and all those outdoorsy things, activities that held no appeal for her whatsoever. As if she wanted to confide a secret, Catherine tilted her head. "He romanticizes what it would be like to settle down and raise a family here, but..." she paused to let her voice firm. "That'll never happen."

She'd barely hidden her shock when Bradley had announced he wanted children. True, they'd never discussed starting a family, but they had their whole future in front of them. If and when they decided to have a baby, that decision was years down the road. She couldn't afford to take that much time off right now. Not when she was at the top of her game. Not when producers and screenwriters begged her to read their scripts and star in their films.

"No?" Sarah's hand found her waist.

"Well, once he's back on tour, jet-setting around the world, he'll forget about this place like he did before and..." she shrugged, "never look back."

Not that there was much to forget. She wouldn't last a week crammed into Bradley's childhood home. Why, it wasn't even half the size of her house in California. With only two bedrooms, where would her staff, her assistants, her agent sleep? And those closets—miniscule didn't even begin to describe them. So, no. She and Bradley definitely weren't moving here.

She glanced down. Alerted by a slight frown that creased Sarah's brow, she hurried to explain the facts of the life she'd been raised to expect. "He has a gift. Something he needs to share with the world. You understand that, right?"

"I do."

"He is extraordinary," she whispered. Bradley was one of the most talented people she'd ever met. Fame and fortune filled his future. For both their sakes, she wouldn't let him throw it all away to live in some tiny backwater town that didn't even have a decent restaurant. A move, she was dead certain, Sarah had planted in his brain. Which brought her to the point of this little meeting. She cleared her throat. "He's very concerned about you."

Catherine plucked a slip of paper from the bag she wore over one arm. The time had come to put all those acting classes to use. This was the role of a lifetime. She wouldn't botch it. In her best sympathy-coated tone, she commiserated with Bradley's childhood sweetheart. "He told me about your financial troubles, and I have a friend in the business. Wonderful man. There's his name and address." She pressed the scribbled note into Sarah's hands. "He takes in horses and other animals that have retired from TV and films. I called him thinking maybe he could help. And he can." Her voice dropped. "He has room to take your horses if you need a place to put them."

She paused to gauge Sarah's reaction. The relieved smile that spread across the other woman's face told her all she needed to know, even without the tears that welled in Sarah's eyes. She'd hit her mark. Putting the rest of her plan into play, Catherine spoke quickly. "In fact, he'd like to talk to you about working on his ranch in California, if you might be interested."

"That's amazing." Sarah gave her head a shake as if she was having a hard time accepting that all this unexpected good luck had fallen into her lap.

"It's serendipitous," Catherine declared. Especially since an entire continent stretched between California and Bradley's Nashville home. "I think you should grab the opportunity and talk to him...right away."

"Well, uh..."

She'd expected Sarah to hesitate. What woman wouldn't stop to reconsider moving away from her friends, her home? But, according to what she'd heard, Sarah had as good as lost her ranch already. As for her friends, she'd make new ones. Catherine dipped her fingers again into the bag crafted of fine, Himalayan leather. What had the salesman called it? Alligator? Crocodile? Something as equally rare and precious as the relationship she shared with Bradley. The one she refused to let him discard. Instead of a slip of paper, this time she retrieved a small package. "I hope you'll accept this, as a gift from Bradley and me. We want to thank you for working so hard to put our wedding together."

The truth was, Bradley had no idea about the arrangement, but that didn't matter. What mattered was that she was doing this as much for him as she was for herself. "I had my assistant book you on a flight for tomorrow morning," she announced. The slim red box tied with a white ribbon dangled from her fingers like a carrot.

A rewarding mix of surprise and gratitude filled Sarah's eyes. "This is very sweet of you."

"You'll have to miss the wedding." Wearing the same sad frown that had tugged on the heartstrings of her fans in countless movies, she delivered the one argument guaranteed to sway a woman who took in stray animals. "But that's not as important as saving your horses. Is it?" She relinquished the gift into Sarah's waiting hands.

"No. No, of course not." Sarah gazed in wonder at the red box. "Thank you very much for doing this."

"A friend of Bradley's is a friend of mine."

She'd done it! With Sarah out of the way, she and Bradley could proceed with the wedding, fly to Italy for their big celebration, and resume the lives they were meant to lead. She faked a smile filled with reassurance for her new best friend while, inside, her heart turned cartwheels. The goal achieved, she headed back the way she'd come.

"Catherine!"

She turned slowly. Had Sarah seen through her generous gesture to the motivation behind it? But no, the rancher only gazed at her with open admiration.

"What's your favorite flower?" Sarah asked.

Catherine threaded her fingers together. "Yellow roses. Why?"

"No reason." Sarah shrugged. Without saying another word, she returned to the horse she'd been tending to and rested her forehead against its broad neck.

Catherine gave the woman a pitying glance. All

in all, she'd have to say that Sarah had nailed the farm hand look. A look she'd try to mimic if she ever accepted a movie role featuring a down-on-her-luck rancher. Her steps quickening, she headed back to the house. She had no idea how long Bradley's errand would take, but the last thing she wanted was for him to see her talking with the woman who'd soon be out of his life completely. Thanks to her.

A line of ants marched single-file across the floorboards of the old fort, while birds flitted among the tree branches overhead. Beyond the tall trunks, puffy white clouds floated in a blue sky. A rustling noise in the bushes alerted Bradley to his friend's arrival. His feet dangling beyond the walls of the tree house that had seemed so large when they were kids, Bradley braced himself against a moss-covered 2x4.

"Thanks for meeting me here," he said when Adam's shoes struck the stairs.

"Glad you called." Though he didn't fit into it as well as he once had, Adam claimed his old spot in the corner. "You okay?"

"Yeah." At least, he thought so. The truth was, he'd never felt more content with his life than he had since his return to Mill Town. Reconnecting with old friends, rediscovering his roots had grounded him somehow, made him more aware of what he valued most in life. He'd been stunned to find that he was more comfortable surrounded by childhood memories In his parents' small home than he'd ever been wandering around the professionally decorated rooms of his big house on the outskirts of Nashville. Discovering that fame and fortune didn't matter as much as he'd thought they did had freed him to write the kind of music he loved without worrying about whether or not his latest songs would climb the charts.

But Catherine wasn't nearly as impressed with all the changes he'd made in his life. In fact, she'd mentioned several times that she couldn't wait till they jetted off to Italy and resumed their "real" lives. Except, he didn't want to go back to the way things were before, and she didn't seem to understand or accept that about him. All of which had led him to seek advice about their relationship, their future, from Adam.

Knowing that his friend's time was valuable, he skipped the usual chit-chat. "How do people look when they're in love? And how do they know they've chosen the right person? The one they're supposed to be with forever."

Adam's chest expanded with the weight of the question. He unfolded the hands he'd propped on one knee. "Well, the bride gets this look in her eyes when she knows she's doing the right thing. She walks into the church. She looks across the room at the groom, and she's got these tears in her eyes. Like she can't see anybody else. She's lost in the moment." A tender smile played across his lips.

"And that's it." *Just a look?* There had to be more to

it than that. Wasn't there a test a couple could take? Or a questionnaire they could fill out that would prove they'd chosen the right mate? He wanted, needed something definitive, something concrete.

"Bradley. The question really is, do you love her?" Adam stared at him, expecting an answer.

"Of course! I mean, she's done so much for me, for my career." Catherine had introduced him to all the right people, helped him smooth and polish his rough edges, shown him how to dress like a star, how to handle himself in a crowd. He owed her so much for all that.

"But do you love her?" Insistent, demanding, Adam's voice cut through all the static.

Bradley took a second to gather his thoughts. Did he love Catherine? He definitely liked her. He certainly respected her. In most ways, they were compatible. He slapped his hands together. "Yes. I love her." He had to, didn't he?

"You're sure this is what you want to do?"

He took a breath. Catherine had assured him that once he left Mill Town behind, once he took his new songs into the studio, once he stepped on stage in Yakima or Orlando or Kalamazoo, he'd realize he'd made the right choice. He had to trust that she knew what she was talking about. Besides, it was too late to call off the wedding, even if he wanted to. Not without embarrassing Catherine, and he wouldn't do that to her. She deserved better than that. "I am. Yeah."

"So, I guess I'll see you at the wedding rehearsal."

Bradley shook out a controlled breath. "Yeah."

"Okay." Carefully ducking the spider webs that clung to the makeshift roof overhead, Adam stood.

"Thanks." Bradley tapped his friend on the shoulder. Who would have guessed, all those years ago, that he'd be the one who asked for advice from the young boy who'd presided over his first wedding?

"You bet."

On his way back to the house, Bradley chewed thoughtfully on Adam's words. In a matter of hours, he'd stand beside his friend and watch as his bride-to-be walked down the aisle to meet him. Warmth spread through his chest. He couldn't wait to see their love for one another reflected in her eyes when Catherine looked at him.

# Chapter Sixteen

Sarah tucked the last of the yellow roses into the small aluminum buckets she and Bradley had purchased from the feed store. She'd been so surprised when he'd suggested using them for the wedding. He'd had no idea that she'd picked out the same kind of pail to show him, and they'd laughed about being in sync.

A stray tear spilled from one of her eyes. She smeared it onto her cheek. She was going to miss being around Bradley. She'd enjoyed their talks. Listening to him work on his music in the evenings had lifted her spirits. But he'd made his choice, and it wasn't her. Though he and Catherine didn't share the deep, abiding love Sarah felt was crucial to any lasting relationship, he was going through with the wedding. And though it broke her heart, she had to respect his decision. He hadn't left her any choice.

She brushed pollen from her hands while she surveyed her handiwork. Each of the dozen containers on her dining room table held an array of chrysanthemum, baby's breath, and the yellow roses she'd picked after talking to Catherine this morning. She plucked a dead leaf from one arrangement, added an extra blossom to another, and managed a smile. The flowers were beautiful, perfect for the simple barn wedding Bradley had asked her to plan.

She almost wished she'd be there to see it, but the opportunity Catherine had sprung on her was simply too good to pass up. Besides, Bradley no longer wanted her at his wedding. If he did, he'd never have let Catherine book that particular flight. Not that she had any interest in watching Bradley marry a woman he didn't love. Why put herself through that heartbreak? And then there were her horses. How would she ever live with herself if they suffered because she refused Catherine's offer? She couldn't. Not when she had the chance to secure their future by skipping the wedding and taking a job in California. No, this was one time she had to agree with Catherine—meeting with the rancher on the West Coast was the right thing, the only thing, to do.

But first, she'd honor her promise to provide the flowers for Bradley's wedding. A quick glance at the clock above the stove told her she had just enough time before the rehearsal to place her arrangements in the barn. Drawing in a steady breath, she gathered up an armload of the centerpieces. On the back porch, she stumbled to a halt.

"What the..." she breathed.

She took in the two immense delivery trucks parked near the barn's wide entrance and the army of workers who swarmed the area. From her vantage point, she spotted rows of gilt chairs which young women busily swathed in white fabric. Other helpers carried armloads of material and flowers through the open barn doors. Her stomach did a slow, uncomfortable tuck-and-roll. Had Bradley approved this, or was it all Catherine's doing?

The idea that he was in the dark about the change in decor—and possibly other things as well—took root as she carried the first batch of flowers down the steps. On the threshold of the barn, she studied the massive bouquets of yellow roses arrayed in tall, crystal vases on either side of a pulpit that had materialized out of thin air. More roses dripped from garlands that had been hung from the rafters. Ivy obscured the support beams. Swags of white tulle camouflaged the walls and stalls. Bile rose in her throat.

What had become of the simple, heartfelt, *honest* ceremony she'd helped plan?

"Oh, Bradley," she whispered as disappointment clogged her throat with tears, "is this the life you really want?" Shaking her head, she placed her modest pots of flowers at the end of every row.

She had to be sure. Had to see his reaction to the fancy white draperies, the crystal chandeliers hanging from the rafters, the bridge someone had built over the goat pens. If he was okay with all the changes, then she'd know she'd lost him forever.

"Okay, let's get started." Adam's voice echoed from the wooden roof.

His head still reeling from the transformation that had been worked on the barn, Bradley swallowed. While he'd be the first to acknowledge that all the white fabric and fancy gilt gave the rustic structure a polished look, the effect wasn't at all what he'd had in mind when he and Sarah had planned his wedding to Catherine.

He searched for the friend who'd stayed out of sight the last few days. Not for the first time since Catherine's arrival, he wished he and Sarah could just talk like they had when they'd worked on her fences.

"Bradley, hop to." Adam pointed to the vacant spot beside him.

He squared his shoulders. Whatever questions he had, they'd have to wait until after the rehearsal. Careful not to trip over a long white runner he'd never seen before, he crossed brand-new flooring that covered the straw-covered aisle and mounted the steps onto a dais he'd swear hadn't existed the last time he'd been in the barn.

"All right. You'll stand here next to me. Face this way. And Catherine..." Adam's focus shifted to the bride who'd rejected his suggestion to follow tradition and have a stand-in take her place during the practice. He gestured toward the back of the building. "When the music starts, cross that bridge, go down that row, and then you'll walk down the aisle toward Bradley."

"Got it." Catherine stepped out of sight.

Bradley blinked as his fiancée disappeared behind an acre of gauzy white fabric that spilled from the rafters. How had Catherine pulled all this off? Better yet, why? She'd said she'd ordered a few things to make their wedding more comfortable, but the lengths she'd gone to had the opposite effect on him. He grew more nervous and uncertain by the minute. Was this what people meant when they talked about cold feet?

"Okay. Let's try this," Adam ordered.

Bradley's hands fisted when a string quartet played the opening notes of "Spring," the first movement in Vivaldi's "Four Seasons." What had happened to the band he and Sarah had chosen? He ground his back teeth together. He didn't like the other *improvements* Catherine had made to his wedding plans, but this one really rankled. Music was his forte, his livelihood. If the band he'd chosen wasn't good enough for his bride, how would *he* ever live up to her expectations?

Beside him, Adam cleared his throat. Suddenly aware that Catherine had emerged through the curtain and had started across the bridge, Bradley straightened. This was it. The moment he and Adam had discussed in the old fort. What did it matter whether his fiancée had decorated the old barn to suit her fancy or not? Or that she'd overruled his selection of the music? None of that counted nearly as much as seeing the love Adam had spoken of reflected in Catherine's eyes. In a matter of seconds, she'd step into the aisle and walk toward him. All his doubts and concerns were sure to fade away the moment their eyes met. Then, he'd know for sure he'd made the right choice.

The music swelled. Her steps sure and certain despite the three-inch heels she wore, Catherine made the turn onto the aisle. Bradley's heart rose to his throat. He gazed intently at his bride, determined not to miss the instant when he'd stare deeply into her brown eyes, and he'd know—they'd both know—their love would withstand every test life threw at it.

Two steps down the aisle, Catherine's footsteps slowed.

Bradley's stomach tightened. His pulse, which had been galloping like one of Sarah's thoroughbreds, stilled. His eyes glued to Catherine, he watched her pull a small mirror from the center of her bouquet, strike a pose, and check her image in the mirror. She nodded her approval. Once more burying the glass in the flowers, she adjusted her veil and, without a single glance his way, flounced down the aisle. Like any good actress, she hit her mark precisely.

Bradley expelled a long, unsteady breath. What had he been thinking? He'd known from the very start that love—romantic love—didn't factor into his feelings for Catherine. Theirs was a relationship based on mutual admiration and respect, common goals and similar drives. For a split second there, he'd hoped for something more, something deeper. But what they had was enough.

Or was it?

A slight movement off to one side caught his

attention. He peered beyond the swags of white fabric into the shadows. His breath caught when he glimpsed Sarah standing there, watching him. Love and heartbreak swirled across her face, and he felt the answering pull of emotion in his chest. In that moment, he wanted to rush to her side, brush away her tears, and spend the rest of his life with her. Only…

He was about to marry Catherine. It was too late for him and Sarah. If he'd never left Mill Town, if he'd returned sooner, if he'd met Sarah some other time, some other place, then, maybe, the make-believe wedding they'd held as kids might have turned into something real, something that would last a lifetime. But now, it was too late. Their chance—if they'd ever had one—had passed.

The sense of loss that swept through him was so powerful it nearly knocked him off his feet. Righting himself, he sought understanding in Sarah's gaze. When their eyes met again, she smiled at him despite the tears that trailed down her cheeks. In that instant, he knew that, like him, she accepted their fate. The forgiveness he read in her expression dissolved the hard knot that had filled the center of his chest ever since their last argument.

Beside him, Adam thumbed the pages of a well-worn Bible. Aware that everyone waited expectantly for him, Bradley straightened. Turning, he faced his bride and carried out his part in their wedding rehearsal. The next time he risked a glance toward the place where he'd spotted Sarah, she had disappeared.

# Chapter Seventeen

Shortly after sunrise, Sarah toted her overnight bag down the wide front steps of the house she'd lived in practically her entire life. Pausing on the bottom stair, she gave the flower garden where she'd spent countless hours a final glance.

No, not final. She wasn't leaving for good. Not yet. Though her ownership of the house and the ranch would end the moment she handed the deed over to James Fargo, she'd return in a few days to get the rest of her clothes and personal items.

But things would never be the same. After today, someone else would pick the flowers she'd so carefully tended. Someone new would cook breakfast in the roomy kitchen where her family had prepared countless meals. People she didn't know would ride on horseback through the fields and woods. They'd be the ones who put their horses in the stalls at night, not her.

For the briefest of moments, she'd hoped things might turn out differently after all. There'd been a minute during the wedding rehearsal yesterday when she'd sworn Bradley realized he was making a huge mistake by marrying Catherine. She'd held her breath, certain he was about to call the whole thing off. But he hadn't. As much as it hurt, she'd had no choice but to accept that she and Bradley weren't meant to be together. That he'd chosen Catherine. That the sooner she accepted it, the sooner she could get on with her life.

Gathering up her courage, she took one long last look at the ranch while it was still hers to enjoy. When she was finally certain the memories of her childhood home would sustain her for the next few days, she toted her overnight bag to the waiting taxi and the driver who lingered by the picket fence.

"I need to make a quick stop at the bank on our way to the airport." She thumbed through her purse, double-checking that she had her wallet and ID.

"Going to be away long?" Sammy stashed her bag in the trunk.

"I'll be back on Friday." She took her place in the back seat. "Do you mind picking me up?"

"Sure thing." Sliding behind the wheel, Sammy grabbed a clipboard from under the visor and jotted down her flight information.

Slumped in her seat, she stared out the window as Sammy followed the road that led through the ranch she loved to a future far different from the one she'd hoped to live. At the bank, she asked the driver to keep the motor running. "I won't be long," she assured him.

As he'd promised, James Fargo greeted her the moment she stepped into the lobby.

"Hi, James." Her shoulders back, her head held high, she refused to give into her tears. She wouldn't plead for another extension. She wouldn't beg or make a scene. She'd promised James she'd hand the deed over to him, and she'd keep her word.

"Hi, Sarah." His manner solemn, the banker accepted the paperwork that relinquished her ownership of the ranch. "I'm real sorry about this."

"Yeah. Me, too." Her requests for help had been rejected at every turn. Banks didn't lend money to ranchers who were already behind in their payments. Mortgage companies didn't give extensions when there was no chance of a looming windfall. Not even the Equine Rehabilitation Fund had been willing to lend a hand. She'd exhausted every option, explored every avenue in the hopes that things wouldn't come to this. She had that much to be proud of. Sticking to her word, she clasped James's outstretched hand and gave it a firm shake.

"Thank you."

Not certain how much longer she could hold her tears at bay, she simply nodded and headed for the waiting taxi and the long ride to the airport.

Was her future in California? Only time would tell, but she didn't think it mattered. She wouldn't exactly call living with a broken heart much of a life. How would she survive the next year, much less the next decade, with this empty hole where her heart should be? She leaned her head back on the seat and closed her eyes. Tears seeped between her lids. They dampened her cheeks. She'd had her one shot at true love. She'd never get a second chance.

Bradley rapped on Sarah's front door. The restlessness that had kept him tossing and turning all night flooded back. He rocked back and forth on his heels. What was taking Sarah so long? Unable to wait for her to come to the door, he knocked again. "Hello?"

Still no answer.

"Sarah?" He raised his voice. Moving to the front window, he cupped his hand over the glass and peered inside. "I need to talk to you." He couldn't spend another minute, much less the rest of his life, wondering about the burst of emotion that had passed between them during the rehearsal yesterday. The time had come for them to have a serious discussion, and he wanted—no, he demanded—that they have it now. He rapped loudly on the glass.

"Hello, there!"

Spinning away from the window, Bradley homed in on the owner of a voice that didn't belong to the woman he needed to see. Though she carried a briefcase, Sally's black braids had been stylishly arranged. Her gray dress looked a little too fine for everyday wear. A teasing grin spread across her face. She leaned toward him. "Aren't you supposed to be getting ready for your wedding?"

The wedding could wait. He had far more important matters to attend. "Where's Sarah?"

"Why, she's gone." Sally's thick brows knitted as though this was information he should already possess.

Bradley held out one hand like a stop sign. "Gone? I don't understand." He marched down the steps, his boots striking a ringing thud on each riser. "What do you mean?"

"Well, she no longer owns this ranch." Sally's voice turned as somber as a funeral director's.

"What?" Bradley flew down the last few steps. He hurried across the yard to stand face-to-face with the realty agent. "She would never sell her ranch." Not the land that had been handed down to her by her parents. Not the home that was tied to all her most important memories, her roots. Not after all the work she'd put into fixing up the place. And especially not after she'd sacrificed so much for the horses in her care.

"She didn't have a choice. She simply didn't have enough money to make the mortgage." Sally's voice hitched. "The bank had to sell it. They didn't have a choice, either."

His arms akimbo, Bradley stared at the agent. Sarah, gone? Her ranch, sold? Why hadn't she come to him for help? He'd have given her whatever she needed.

"I'm taking care of the dogs," Sally offered. "But the horses are getting picked up."

This was wrong, just wrong. Sarah had lived here her whole life. She loved the land. Her horses meant more to her than they could ever mean to a stranger. He didn't care how much it cost him, he'd get Sarah's ranch back for her. She'd refused his help once before, but she wasn't here to stop him now. His mind made up, he stated his case. "Well, I'll talk to the people who bought it, and I'll get it back."

An odd mix of confusion and surprise twisted Sally's lips into an unsettling pretzel. Maybe getting Sarah's property back for her wasn't going to be as easy as he'd thought.

Pretty sure he wasn't going to like the answer, he asked, "Who bought the ranch?"

Looking more bewildered than ever, Sally cleared her throat. "You did," she whispered.

"I—" Words failed him.

He'd had a lot of new experiences over the last couple of weeks. In the decade he'd spent away from Mill Town, he'd never once ridden a horse. But he'd brushed up his riding skills since he'd come back. He'd learned how to wield a hammer well enough to mend a fence or fifty, caught his first big trout, enjoyed an ice cream on a lazy afternoon. Most of all, thanks to Sarah, he'd rediscovered the truth of that old adage, "home is where the heart is," and finally figured out that Mill Town was where he belonged.

So, yeah, he'd done a lot of things, but he most certainly hadn't bought a ranch. And definitely not Sarah's—he'd never buy her property out from under her.

A loose, uneasy sensation slid through his belly,

and his thoughts narrowed. While he'd never take Sarah's ranch from her, he knew someone who might have done exactly that.

"Excuse me." He strode toward the house on the hill.

Leaving the realty agent standing in the middle of the lawn with her mouth hanging open wasn't the effect he had on most people, but he and Catherine needed to talk. And right now, before either of them made a mistake they couldn't undo.

Bradley thundered up the steps of the house. At the door, he raised his fist to rap on the wood. He dropped his hand to his side. Why knock? This was his house, wasn't it? Or had Catherine managed to sweep it out from under him like she'd done with Sarah's ranch? He burst into the living room.

At his unexpected presence, hair stylists, dress attendants, and makeup artists froze. Like actors on a set who stood on their marks until someone called, "Action!" they stared at Catherine and waited for her signal.

Looking every bit the reigning queen of the big screen, his bride-to-be sat in a director's chair. Instead of a megaphone, she held a large mirror as her prop. Without bothering to turn toward him, she spoke into the mirror. "You can't come in here," she protested.

"I need to speak to you." His anger at what he suspected she'd done fueled him. He stormed past the frozen attendants.

"You can't see the bride before the wedding." Catherine's voice rose to an uncharacteristic and rather unattractive screech. "It's bad luck!"

Now she was worried about bad luck? Now? She hadn't worried about bad luck during last night's wedding rehearsal. When Adam had suggested they follow tradition by using a stand-in, Catherine had insisted on walking down the aisle herself. She hadn't given a thought to bad luck when she'd put every detail of planning their wedding into his hands while she'd stayed in California. She hadn't blinked an eye when, against his wishes, she'd announced their engagement on national television. Was she really worried about bad luck? He didn't think so. He thought it far more likely that his bride feared he'd stumbled onto her secrets and didn't want to discuss them until it was too late to undo what she'd done.

He stopped just short of her chair. "Did you buy Sarah's ranch?"

Beneath her expertly applied makeup, Catherine's reflection paled. "Okay." She lowered the mirror. Still not glancing at him, she addressed her staff. "Everybody out." A laugh as fake as her nails filled the room. "The groom needs to speak to the bride."

As far as he was concerned, Catherine's assistants couldn't vacate the premises fast enough. Though he wanted to rage, to smash something, he held his tongue while, without a single word, the line of helpers filed out of the room. "It's a simple question, Catherine," he growled when the door closed behind the last of her staff. "Did you, or did you not, buy Sarah's ranch?"

The departure of the would-be witnesses must have given his fiancée the time she needed to get over her initial shock. Nary a tremble shook her fingers as she lay the mirror on the kitchen table that doubled as a makeup stand. Catherine slid from the tall chair, drew herself erect and faced him. "Bradley, I know how much this place means to you." She gestured at the house that had been his home when he was a kid, the one she'd declared far too small for their needs. "And I know you want to keep it."

"What's that have to do with you buying Sarah's ranch?" Determined not to let his anger get the best of him, to give Catherine a chance to explain, he propped his hands on his hips.

"We can expand the property," Catherine gushed, as if her wants and desires justified all the maneuvering she'd done behind his back. "We can build a new house here. A real house. A house we can come back to. A house worthy of people like us."

"People like *us*?" The kind of people who used whatever means necessary to get what they wanted? That wasn't him. He was just an ordinary guy who'd had a few lucky breaks. He retreated a step.

"You know what I mean."

No, he didn't. But he was beginning to. He suspected that, left to her own devices, Catherine would raze both Sarah's place and his, and replace them with a mansion far more suited to Beverly Hills than tiny Mill Town.

Behind him, a bright light flashed. A distinctive click sounded. Then, another flash went off. He spun, his gaze landing on a photographer who crouched near the open door.

"Who the heck is that?" he demanded. Even as he pointed at the man, the guy fired off another series of shots. "Do you mind?" His footsteps as menacing as he could make them, he strode toward the interloper, who had the good sense to dart out the door. Bradley firmly closed it in his wake.

"He's with *People Magazine*." Dismay darkened Catherine's eyes. She stared after the disappearing photographer.

"Are you kidding me?" She had to be joking. She knew how important his privacy was to him.

"Now, I know you didn't want me—"

"We discussed this."

"But he promised he'd be discreet. You won't even notice him."

"Right." Like he hadn't noticed the man snapping pictures in the middle of the most important discussion he'd ever have with Catherine. He took a breath. Over the last year, he'd done everything she'd asked without asking for anything in return. When his bride-to-be had complained that his blue-collar roots showed in his clothes, he'd let her take him shopping for a new wardrobe. They'd attended the parties she chose, sent their regrets to invitations that didn't meet her standards. Most nights, instead of working on his music, he'd accompanied her to swanky restaurants where she could be seen by the movers and shakers in the movie and music industries. He'd even agreed to marry her in Italy and honeymoon in Europe when what he'd really wanted was a week-long getaway in a secluded cabin in the woods.

In all that time, he'd only asked one thing from Catherine: that their wedding be a private, intimate moment with just the two of them. Yet, not only had she announced their engagement on national TV, she'd invited the press to attend the ceremony without the slightest regard for what he wanted.

What did that mean for their future? He stared at Catherine. Did she really consider her wants, her needs to be that much more important than everyone else's?

Granted, Catherine was extremely talented, and she'd worked hard to get where she was today. But other people had talents, too, didn't they? Adam's sermons could move his congregation to tears. James Fargo ran the Mill Town Bank with compassion and care. Sally Hartford had such a big heart that she took care of her clients' dogs when they were out of town. Sammy Harper and his band might never make it to Nashville, but they had every foot in the Mill Town Bar tapping on Friday nights. And what about him? Maybe he could perform better than most, but he'd be perfectly content as long as he had a roof over his head, an old pickup truck to ride around in, and a fishing pole.

But not Catherine. She thrived on the limelight. Stardom was in her blood. He took a breath. Okay, maybe he'd pushed her too hard, tried to force a city girl to adopt his country ways without giving her time to adjust. Much as he hated to admit it, he had sprung the idea of living in his childhood home on her without even asking her about it. Oh, he'd had the best of intentions. He'd thought he could introduce her to the simpler things—the house where he'd grown up, life in a small town, the pleasures of country living—and she'd discover they meant the same to her as they did to him.

But he'd been wrong. He saw that now. Catherine would never find the joy in fixing a home-cooked meal. She'd never settle for dinner at the Mill Town Diner on Friday night or meeting friends for an evening of line dancing on Saturday. Any more than he'd ever be content to live the rest of his life in the city.

Why had he ever thought their lives were compatible?

As if she sensed the direction his thoughts had taken and wanted to distract him, Catherine brushed passed him. "I love all the flowers for the wedding." Her bouquet rested atop the mantle. She cupped her fingers around the petals. "How did you know that yellow roses were my favorite?"

"I didn't." He hadn't known her favorite flower any more than he'd known which color she preferred, whether she liked chocolate or strawberry, or that coconut gave her hives. Nor had he known she'd go behind his back and ruin a friend's life to get what she wanted. "Sarah must have known. You know, that ranch is her home. She's lived there her entire life." For Catherine to strip that away from Sarah, well, he wasn't sure he'd ever forgive her for that.

"I think it's so sweet that you still care about her." Reaching for him, Catherine trailed her fingers along his collar bone. "It's one of the reasons I love you so much."

He stumbled back a half-step. Though Catherine was saying the right things, her words struck one false note after another. They'd both agreed that their relationship wasn't based on love. Now, when she had to sense how badly she'd disappointed him, she claimed she loved him. Did she even know what the word meant?

Trust, friendship, and support were the ingredients that made love possible. He'd explained how important Sarah was to him, that he wanted the two women to be friends. Apparently, his opinion hadn't mattered to his fiancée. If it had, she'd have moved heaven and earth to help Sarah keep her ranch. Instead of supporting his wish to get married in the old barn, she'd given the entire building a Hollywood-style makeover and brought in caterers. She'd assured him that their ceremony in Italy would be a simple exchange of vows where the world couldn't find them. But considering the presence of the photographer from *People Magazine*, could he even trust Catherine to keep her word?

That was what it all boiled down to, didn't it? He didn't trust Catherine. Not to keep her word about the ceremony in Italy. Not to consider his wishes. Not to put their marriage above what was best for her career.

How could he marry someone he didn't trust? Someone who didn't support him? Who'd gone out of her way to undermine his best friend? The plain fact of the matter was, he couldn't.

He brushed her hand from his chest. "I can't marry you."

Looking at him as if he'd lost his marbles, Catherine tilted her head. "I'm sorry?"

"I can't marry you." He couldn't say it much plainer than that.

"Of course you can."

He chose to overlook the steely glint in her eyes. "Do you love me?"

Catherine scoffed. "Of course I do."

"Why?"

"Because we're perfect for each other. We understand each other. We want the same things."

No, no, and no. They weren't perfect for each other. She didn't understand him. And they sure as heck didn't want the same things. He didn't want the same kind of life she wanted. He was pretty sure he never had. Not really. Down deep in his soul, he'd always known things weren't going to work out between him and Catherine. It had just taken him a long time to see it. To know his own mind. To realize what was important to him. Now that he did, he was going to hold onto it.

"I'm not going to tour for a while. I'm going to live here. Play locally. Build a studio. And write music." There. He'd laid it all out for her.

"That's so silly," she protested. "Your career's on fire. You're gaining momentum. You're—"

"Catherine!" This had to end. "I care about you. I do. But it's just not enough." Not enough to spend the rest of their lives together. "I'm sorry."

That part was truer than she'd ever know. But they both deserved better than a loveless marriage. And, having said his piece, he covered the distance to the door in five quick strides. He'd leave it up to her how she wanted to break the news to the world. He had no doubt she'd place the blame squarely on his shoulders. If it made her feel better, so be it. He had broad shoulders. He'd take the hit.

At the hitching post, he mounted the horse he'd ridden to Sarah's earlier. She might have lied about a lot of things, but one thing Catherine had said rang true. He cared about Sarah. In fact, his feelings for her played a huge role in his certainty that Catherine and he hadn't been meant for each other. If they were, he wouldn't still be thinking of Sarah, would he?

He needed time to think about what to do next. Where he was headed. What—and who—he wanted in his life. And galloping across the fields on horseback, the rush of wind in his face, the muscles of a powerful animal lengthening and retracting beneath him—well, he couldn't think of a better place to do it.

At the top of a hill overlooking green fields and forest, Bradley reined his horse to a stop. It was time to discard the old and move on with the new. If he was going to do this, move back to Mill Town permanently, build a studio and concentrate on writing new music, the trappings of the career he'd thought he wanted would only weigh him down. The hat his agent had given him rested heavily on his head. Removing it, he sailed the ridiculously expensive Stetson into the bushes.

*There.* He gathered the reins into his hands. He felt better already.

# Chapter Eighteen

"**W**elcome home, Sarah." Sammy grabbed her overnight bag from the taxi's front seat. Rounding the rear bumper, he lingered while she counted out a dwindling pile of bills.

"Well, thanks, Sam. But it's not home anymore." She handed across the fare plus the most generous tip she could afford. "I'm just here to pack up."

"Oh. I see." Sammy tucked the money in a pocket. "Where will you go?"

"I don't know." Sarah squinted into the sun. Sammy's question was one of many she faced and couldn't answer. She wouldn't head to California. That was one thing she was certain of. Things hadn't exactly turned out as advertised with Catherine's friend. Though he'd been willing enough to take her horses, the promised job offer had never materialized. Not that she would have taken it if it had. Desert cacti and a scorching dry heat weren't for her. After only two days in the arid climate, she missed trees and green grass and rolling hills too much to linger on the West Coast a minute longer than absolutely necessary.

Across the yard, brilliant colors sparkled from her flower garden. She drew in a floral-scented breath. James Fargo had given her a week to pack up her personal belongings and move out of the house. After that, finding a place to live and a job came next. If she was lucky, she'd land one that would put her veterinary skills to good use.

"I'm sorry." Sammy's head hung low.

"Yeah, thanks, Sam." Pulling her wheeled bag behind her, she started up the walkway to the house. "See you around."

Crossing the threshold, she whistled for the dogs. They came at her at a dead run, slipping and sliding across the hardwood floors in their eagerness to get to her.

"Hi! Hi, guys!" She squatted down low for the usual outpouring of slobbery kisses. "It's so good to see you. I missed you so much."

Normally the dogs were so glad to see her after a trip they lolled about the floor, begging for tummy rubs. This time, though, she barely had a chance to say hello before, barking excitedly, the golden retriever took off for the kitchen. The sheepdog and the cocker spaniel joined in the chase, and soon all three dogs raised a noisy ruckus at the back of the house.

"Kelly, what are you barking at?" Abandoning her luggage, she followed the pack into the kitchen. "What's going on?" she called when Kelly pawed at the door knob while Cooper whined at the window. She peered through the glass into the back yard. Had deer wandered into the garden? She shook her head. Other than a couple of missing catering and delivery trucks, which had probably headed back to the city right after the wedding, everything was exactly as it had been when she left. "What's going on, you guys?"

Hoping to find out what had the dogs so stirred up, she opened the door. The instant she did, Kelly shot past her. Long hair streaming behind her, the retriever bounded down the steps with the other two dogs nipping at her heels. All three of them raced through the flower garden and out of sight. Sarah hustled after them.

"Where are you guys going?" Her long strides covered the ground while concern shifted in her chest. Any number of wild animals had wandered out of the woods in the past. Most would head back in the direction they'd come as soon as the dogs neared, but she couldn't stand the thought of what might happen if her pets cornered a bear or a snake. She raised her voice. "What got into you? Kelly!"

At last, the retriever came to a sliding halt at the barn. Barking for all she was worth, the dog sat on her haunches. While the other two raced back the way they'd come, Kelly whined and pawed at the massive door.

"What you got there?" Sarah tsked. One of the caterers must have pulled the door shut by mistake. She tugged at the handle. Two stories tall, the heavy wooden door didn't budge. She put some muscle into her efforts and was rewarded when the opening widened.

Perplexed at movement inside the barn, she stepped aside as Adam appeared out of the shadows. "I'll get that," he offered. He pushed the door out of the way.

Suddenly, people spilled through the opening. Sarah scanned the group, noting the faces of friends and acquaintances from town. A dry laugh escaped her as unease bubbled in her stomach. No wonder the dogs had gone crazy. It wasn't every day that a crowd chose to gather in her barn. Why were they there? She ventured a tentative, "Hi?" and looked around for someone who could explain what was going on.

Her pulse quickened when Bradley appeared in the midst of the group. When he started toward her, people stepped aside to let him pass. His steps sure and focused, he covered the distance between them.

Her thoughts swam. Even more confused by the appearance of the man who should be on his honeymoon in Europe, she blinked. "What is going on?" Her gaze locked on Bradley, she asked, "Did you decide to have the wedding today?" She swept a glance over the crowd of people in their Sunday best. "Where's Catherine?"

"I'm not sure." Bradley's starched white shirt stretched across his chest. A long-suffering sigh stuttered across his lips.

She folded her arms. None of this was making any sense. "I don't understand."

Bradley brushed the brim of a black cowboy hat. "Well, I was thinking we could renew our vows."

Her heart thumped. *Our* vows? Not his and Catherine's? "What?"

"We got married when we were kids." In a move she'd seen him make whenever he was uncertain, Bradley slipped his hands into his pockets. "I think that was our one chance at true love."

"True love, huh?" She searched Bradley's face for some sign that this was all a big practical joke. Not that she expected to find anything there. He'd never been a trickster. Beneath the dark cowboy hat she'd chosen the day they'd picked out his tux, his eyes glinted with a somber gravity. Was this for real, then? Afraid to trust her heart, she hid her hopes, her dreams beneath a mocking tone. "Well, I don't know. That's romantic. Not realistic."

"I agree. It's rare." Bradley swallowed. His gaze bore into hers. "But I don't want to settle for less."

Surely, he didn't mean... Her heart gave another painful thud. "You don't?"

She searched for truth in his eyes and lost herself in the love she found in his tender smile. She held her breath when he leaned closer. His strong fingers squeezed her shoulders.

"Mint chip." Bradley's eyes captured hers.

Despite the thirteen years they'd spent apart, he'd never forgotten.

"Blue."

The color filled her closet, her house.

"Horses…and dogs."

One of her rescues whinnied from a stall. At her feet, Kelly barked.

"White lilies."

She sucked in a breath. Tears burned the back of her throat. He really did know her.

"This ranch." He cast a look behind him. "And these people," he finished.

Though tears threatened, she smiled past them. She nodded. "They're all my favorite things." He knew her so well.

His gaze captured hers and never wavered as Bradley swept his hat from his head and tucked it under one arm. "I love you with all of my heart. And I want to walk through life leaning against you, so that neither one of us falls. You…are my true love."

Not so long ago, she'd said those very words to him. That day, she would have sworn he hadn't been listening. But she couldn't have been more wrong. He'd heard her every word and committed them all to memory. She ached to tell him how much the gesture meant to her, but the emotion that swelled in her chest made it impossible to speak. Instead, she let her eyes do her talking for her. Her gaze locked on the man she'd fallen in love with thirteen years ago, she watched as he reached into the pocket of his jeans and sank down on one knee.

"Sarah Standor. Will you marry me…again?"

This—this was what she'd prayed for, what she'd hoped for. She'd known they were supposed to be together from the very beginning. It had taken Bradley a little while to reach the same conclusion, but he'd done it. How could she do anything but agree?

"Umm-hmmm." Unable to trust her voice, she merely nodded.

Nothing had ever felt so right as it did the moment Bradley slipped the simple diamond that had belonged to his mother on her finger—for real this time. Cheers and applause erupted around them. Friends and neighbors surged forward to share in their happy moment. While Bradley swept her into his arms and twirled her around, her heart finally settled into a steady beat that Sarah knew would last a lifetime.

That evening, Bradley took his place beside Adam. He breathed a sigh of relief as he surveyed the barn. Gone were all the fancy draperies, the fake bridge, the hastily constructed dais Catherine had used to disguise the building. In their place, electric lights cast rosy shadows on the paper doilies that dotted the barn's aged gray walls. Greenery and white flowers climbed the legs of tall ladders and dripped from an overhead arbor. Behind Adam, a sheet of plain white linen covered a makeshift altar. Before them stood the citizens of Mill Town, who'd turned out in force to witness the union of two of its favorite citizens.

He cast a loving glance at Sarah. Wearing the simple white gown she'd picked out in town, she held a bouquet of lilies. A band of white flowers circled her head. She'd never looked more beautiful. When she'd walked down the straw-covered aisle to stand in front of their minister and friend, so much love had filled his heart, he'd thought it might burst.

"Do you, Sarah, promise to love Bradley in sickness and in health, forever and ever?"

"I do." Certainty glinted in her eyes and deepened her smile.

Adam closed his Bible with a finality that seemed appropriate. "I now pronounce you husband and wife." He turned to Bradley. "You may kiss the bride."

This was the moment he'd been waiting for his entire life. He swept his hat from his head. Shoving it into Adam's chest, he moved toward Sarah. He bent low, his intent clear. His lips pressed against hers. He swept her into his arms and held her so close that he felt it when her pulse soared. He hung onto her, prolonging the moment until their hearts beat as one, echoing the promise that they were meant to be together and always had been.

While the crowd in the barn cheered and showered them with flower petals, Sammy's band played the closing verse of his new song about a cowboy who'd finally figured it all out and come back where he belonged. Moments later, he and his bride threaded through the well-wishers to start their new lives together...forever.

# Epilogue

B radley skimmed the tips of his fingers over the brim of the Stetson he'd picked up on his last trip into Mill Town. His hand firmly anchored at Sarah's hip, he guided his bride of sixteen months into the blue circle taped on the floor in front of Stan. The television show host tapped his mic. Just beyond camera range, technicians wearing headsets studied banks of screens. Despite the noise and shouts that echoed off the walls backstage at the Bridgestone Arena, the producer gave the thumbs-up sign. Stan's shoulders straightened. He faced the cameras and bared flawless white teeth in his signature smile.

"I'm coming to you from the Country Music Awards in Nashville, Tennessee, where we're talking with superstar Bradley Suttons." Stan executed a perfect quarter turn as he shifted around to face his guests. "Congratulations on what has to be a huge night for you, Bradley. Not only were you named country music's Best Male Vocalist of the Year, but your album, *Coming Home*, also won the coveted Album of the Year award. That's an incredible achievement for a relative newcomer. Why, you won your first Grammy less than two years ago. Tell us, what's your secret to success?"

Bradley smiled as Stan thrust the mic under his chin. As much as aspiring artists wished they could wave a magic wand and achieve instant stardom, climbing to the top took hard work, determination, and grit. Sure, he'd had a couple of lucky breaks, but none of them had done as much for his career as the woman who stood beside him. Sarah had given him the freedom, the encouragement he needed to write songs from his heart. "I owe my success to this woman right here." He pulled his wife closer. He'd been certain she'd never look more beautiful than on their wedding day, but tonight, with sequins reflecting light from overhead cams onto her face, Sarah glowed with a luminous beauty. "She taught me everything I know about true love, romantic love. She's the inspiration behind the songs on *Coming Home*."

Stan pivoted slightly toward Sarah. His wide smile deepened. "I know country music fans all over the world will agree with me when I say, 'Thank you!'" His focus shifted, and he rubbed his chin. "Bradley, there've been a lot of changes in your life since I last had you on my show, haven't there? I understand you've left Nashville. You're living in Texas now?"

"Yes, that's right, Stan. A little town called Mill Town, where I grew up as a kid. I married the girl next door." He gave Sarah an affectionate squeeze. "I built a recording studio there and hired some talented local musicians to work with me." He nodded to Sammy and smiled when his new bandleader waved in return. "When I'm not in the recording studio, Sarah and I run a refuge for abused and aging horses."

"And I understand you're very hands-on with the project, aren't you?"

"Sarah's in charge. But yes, I do my part." Bradley scuffed a boot against the floorboards. In the year and a half since he and Sarah had combined their ranches, he'd grown accustomed to the horses' velvety snuffle when he fed them their morning carrots. "These intelligent animals have been through so much. We give them a beautiful place to live out their final days, with plenty of food and clean water and, most of all, kindness and love."

A master at keeping an interview on point, Stan steered the conversation back to the topic of the evening. "When you were on stage, you said there were a lot of people who helped make *Coming Home* Album of the Year. Is there anyone in particular you want to mention?"

Bradley took a breath. As he stood before the arena's capacity crowd moments ago, he'd thanked the record company and his band, but there were so many others who deserved his heartfelt appreciation. "Well, Stan, I'd have to say these wins tonight are all because of my fans, my listeners. I owe them all a huge round of thanks. *Coming Home* was a labor of love, and I can't tell you how much it means to me that my listeners love it, too." He hefted one of the two seven-and-a-half-pound crystal trophies. Beside him, Sarah cradled the second trophy like a baby in her arms. "They really earned these awards as much as I did."

"That's right, Bradley. Your record company wasn't happy with *Coming Home* at first, were they?"

"I wouldn't go that far." Bradley lifted one eyebrow as a warning. Stan had wandered ever so slightly off the script that had been reviewed and approved by his publicity team. If the talk show host hoped to have him as a guest in his Hollywood studio in the future, he'd dial it back a bit. "*Coming Home* was different from what they expected. It wasn't what either of us thought I'd deliver. But, as soon as the label started getting all the positive feedback from listeners and radio stations, they knew they had a hit on their hands. Still, we took a big chance with *Coming Home*. It's good to see that all our efforts paid off."

"What's the one thing that made the album such a success?"

The question had come straight from the approved list, and Bradley doffed his hat in acknowledgement. "The theme is so universal. Every song on the album is about discovering what's important in life, finding your roots, understanding that home is where your heart is. And love. What can be better than that?"

"What indeed!"

A round of applause erupted from the stage out front where another star had just received their award. Soon, they'd take their place on the blue circle in front of the next interviewer.

Across the mic, Bradley arched a questioning glance at Sarah. At her answering nod, he turned a warm smile on Stan. The time had come to reward the talk show host with a tidbit of little-known information. He tipped his chin to his wife. "Few people know it, but this is actually our second marriage...to each other. The first time, we were just thirteen. My parents had just died, and Sarah wanted to make sure I had a family, so she married me. I moved to Nashville the next day with my aunt and uncle. A dozen years passed, but that first wedding must have stuck, 'cause when we saw each other again, Sarah and I fell for one another."

Stan's eyes sparkled. "Why, that's one of the sweetest stories I've ever heard. I want to thank you, Bradley and Sarah, for sharing that with me and our listening audience."

Bradley recognized the cue. The interview was drawing to a close. "Again, I want to say thanks to all my fans and listeners. Without you, without your support, these awards would be just two more trophies on my shelf. But they have special meaning because of all the love you've shown me and given *Coming Home*."

Expecting the usual, "You heard it here first," spiel from Stan, he relinquished the mic. Instead of wrapping things up though, the talk show host stared at a spot behind Bradley while an expectant hush spread through the backstage. Bustling assistants paused midstep. Cameras swung in a new direction. Strobe lights flashed.

Bradley caught a warning glance from Sammy and

braced for another troubling detour from the script when Stan cleared his throat.

"Can this night get any better?" Stan raised the mic to his lips. "I see Catherine Mann heading our way. Let's see if we can get her to join us."

*Is that all?* A laugh bubbled in Bradley's chest. No doubt, Stan viewed the star's arrival as an opportunity for a bit of conflict that would boost his ratings even higher. But the joke was on their host. Catherine had been the one who'd schooled him in the art of onscreen diplomacy. She'd never let even the tiniest bit of animosity show during an interview. Not that they had any differences, that was. They'd long since resolved the problems between them.

"Catherine Mann." Stan's sunny smile locked onto his favorite movie star as she slipped her arm free of her escort's. While the tall, dark-haired man lingered in the shadows beyond the camera's angle, she stepped into the circle beside Bradley and Sarah.

"Stan, how wonderful to run into you here." Catherine's amused glance let Bradley know that the run-in was anything but accidental. "I didn't know you were handling the backstage interviews at the CMA's."

"I jumped at the chance to be part of the biggest night of the year in country music." Stan beamed his pleasure in landing the impromptu opportunity to feature two mega stars on his program. "I must say, you're looking especially lovely this evening."

Catherine ran a hand down a beaded white dress that showed off her curves to their best advantage.

Beneath the floodlights, the crystal-studded gown shimmered. "Thanks, Stan. It's Armani, and I do love it so. But I'm not here to talk about me. I stopped by to give my congratulations to Bradley. No one deserves these awards more than he does."

"That's right." Stan snapped his fingers as though a new thought had just occurred to him. "You and Bradley used to be engaged, weren't you?"

"We were, but that was ages ago. We've both moved on." Like a parent admonishing an unruly child, Catherine aimed a stern look at the television host.

"Yes, but I've heard people say there's some kind of feud between the three of you." Stan's eager glance searched their faces. "Isn't it true, Catherine, that you bought Sarah's ranch?"

When the tiniest bit of color crawled up Catherine's neck and onto her cheeks, Bradley sliced a hand through the air. *Enough.* He broke in. "The tabloids would love to portray us as the Hatfields and the McCoys, but that was all a huge misunderstanding."

Catherine straightened the diamond on her left ring finger. "I only bought that land to preserve it for Sarah," she insisted, flawlessly delivering the line they'd all agreed on. "In fact, I signed it over to her, free and clear, as my wedding present to her and Bradley."

Sarah nodded her agreement. "It was the most thoughtful—and the most generous—gift anyone ever gave me."

"So there's no truth to the rumors of bad blood between you?"

"Certainly not," Sarah put in. Shifting the Male Vocalist of the Year award to her other arm, she slipped her hand around Catherine's waist.

"Oh my heavens, we're the best of friends." Catherine gushed. "Why else do you think I asked my producers to consider Bradley's music for the soundtrack in *Simple Pleasures*?" The newly released movie had shattered box office records and earned her an Academy Award nomination.

"Well, there you have it, folks. Contrary to speculation, there's no truth to the rumors of bad blood between Catherine Mann and Bradley Suttons." Stan's hopeful look tightened. "So, Catherine. I understand there's a new man in your life."

In a move that sealed her place in the talk show host's heart, Catherine waved a beckoning hand to the man who stood beyond the circle of camera lights. "Stan, I don't think you've met my fiancé, Warren Barfield. It was love at first sight when we met on the set of *Simple Pleasures*."

Stan's head bobbed in a sign of respect for the movie producer and media mogul. "A pleasure." His eyes gleaming, he tilted his head. "Have you two lovebirds set a date?"

Catherine drew in a breath. Her eyes sparkled. At her side, Warren merely cleared his throat, but the sound immediately stuck a cork in whatever announcement the star had been about to make. She studied the tips of her toes for a beat. When she raised her head, she wore a demure expression. "I'm sorry,

Stan. We haven't finalized our plans yet. When we do though, you'll be the first to know."

*Well, well, well.* From his spot at the end of the foursome, Bradley smothered the urge to shoot Warren a congratulatory grin. The man had done something no one else had been able to do. He'd tamed Catherine's worst impulses.

"I'll hold you to that," Stan said smoothly. He tapped his ear piece. "And we're out," he announced, his shoulders sagging. An assistant dashed forward and began removing wires, receivers, and ear buds from under his suit coat. While the young woman worked, Stan gave handshakes all around. "Thank you all for that awesome talk. My viewers are sure to love it when it airs in the morning. I'd rather stick around and chat, but my producer just informed me that our limo is waiting outside and blocking traffic. I'll catch you later at the after parties. Gotta run." He handed his mic to the assistant and took off on a loping walk.

Bradley extended a hand to the man who owned his record company and a half-dozen television stations. "Mr. Barfield, I don't think we've been formally introduced. I'm Bradley Suttons, and this is my wife, Sarah."

"Warren. It's a pleasure," replied Catherine's fiancé while they exchanged firm handshakes. He eyed the twin trophies. "And congratulations."

Bradley took a second to bask in the praise from one of the most powerful men in the entertainment industry. No matter what the future held, nothing would top the excitement of this night. "It's quite an honor."

Catherine peered coquettishly at her beau. "Can I tell them?"

A twinkle came into Warren's eyes. "Yes, of course. We just don't want it blasted all over the headlines."

"You're right." Turning to face Bradley and Sarah, Catherine smiled sweetly. "Warren's been helping me learn how to handle the press a little better." She cleared her throat. "We weren't exactly truthful with Stan. We *have* set a date. We're getting married next month. December first, at Warren's estate in Napa Valley. We both would love it if you'd come."

Bradley gave Sarah a questioning look and noted her slight nod. "We wouldn't miss it."

Behind her hand, his wife yawned. "Oh, sorry." She checked the time on the diamond-studded watch he'd given her on their first anniversary. "I'm used to getting up before daybreak to feed and water the horses. It's way past my usual bedtime."

"Does that mean you won't be coming to the Warner Music After-Party?" Disappointment clouded Catherine's eyes. The bash was *the* event of the year. All the country music legends would be there.

Sarah spoke for them, "I'm afraid not. We—the three of us—are heading back to the hotel. We have an early flight to catch."

Bradley traded an indulgent smile with Catherine's beau. Even for veterans of performances and awards ceremonies, the long day of fittings and preparations for tonight's gala extracted a toll. Sarah, a newcomer to all the fuss, had become so exhausted that she'd miscounted. Intending to lighten her load, he shifted one of the heavy trophies in order to take the one she held. The four of them—Sarah and him, along with his trophies—would spend the night in their comfy hotel suite before heading home tomorrow.

On the other side of their little circle, Catherine gasped. "You're—" The mega star's voice trailed off.

"She's...what?" Bradley studied his wife while a thousand disasters flashed through his mind.

Beside him, Sarah smiled a secretive smile. Her fingers trailed over a slight bulge below her waist.

Suddenly, pieces of a puzzle he hadn't realized he was trying to solve fell into place. Sarah's luminous glow. The way she'd cradled his trophy. Her fatigue. Her recent bout with a stomach virus. The picture of a cradle swam into view. Lullabies rang through his head. Images of playing catch in the backyard, going to dance recitals, first dates, and high school graduations flashed before his eyes.

His fingers lost their grip on the crystal trophy. When it slipped from his hands, only Catherine's quick reactions saved it from shattering into a million pieces. He peered into Sarah's face, where the truth shone like a beacon. Nothing, not even winning two CMA awards, meant as much to him as the glow he saw in her eyes.

His heart bursting, he lifted Sarah off her feet and hugged her close while he marveled at the spur-of-the-moment decision that had changed his life. He'd returned to Mill Town to let go of the past. But instead of letting go, he'd found his true love, his roots, the place he belonged forever. Thanks to that one twist of fate, he was the luckiest man in the world.

"Let's go home," he whispered into Sarah's hair. And together, they walked out of the Bridgestone Arena and headed for Mill Town and the simple life they'd built on a ranch where their hearts would always beat as one.

# "Bradley Sutton" Cowboy Steak Sandwiches

*A Hallmark Original Recipe*

In *Country Wedding*, Bradley and Sarah stop at the Milltown Family Diner for lunch. "We will have two Bradley Sutton Sandwiches," says Sarah. This hearty grilled steak sandwich with white cheddar, onions, and horseradish mayo would be a hit on any menu.

**Yield:** 2 sandwiches
**Prep Time**: 15 minutes
**Cook Time:** 30 minutes
**Total Time:** 45 minutes

## INGREDIENTS

Horseradish Mayonnaise:
- ¼ cup mayonnaise
- 1 teaspoon horseradish sauce
- ¼ teaspoon garlic and pepper seasoning

Caramelized Onions:
- 1 tablespoon olive oil
- 1 yellow onion, cut length-wise into - ¼-inch slices
- ¼ teaspoon each: kosher salt and black pepper

- 1 (1½-inch thick) boneless ribeye steak, room temperature
- as needed, kosher salt and black pepper
- 1 tablespoon olive oil
- 2 tablespoons unsalted butter, room temperature
- 2 crusty sandwich rolls (sourdough, Kaiser or onion rolls), warm
- 1 cup spring mix salad greens
- ¼ cup white sharp Cheddar cheese, shredded

## DIRECTIONS

1. To prepare horseradish mayonnaise: combine mayonnaise, horseradish and garlic pepper in

small bowl and stir to blend. Taste and adjust seasoning, if desired.

2. To prepare caramelized onions: heat oil in a large skillet over medium heat; add onions, salt and black pepper. Cook for 2 to 3 minutes, stirring frequently, or until onions are wilted. Reduce heat to medium-low and cook for 15 to 20 minutes, stirring frequently, or until onions are golden and lightly caramelized.

3. Meanwhile, heat a cast iron skillet over high heat until very hot (about 5 minutes). Remove excess moisture on steak with paper towels; season steak generously with salt and black pepper. Add oil to hot skillet; heat until just beginning to smoke. Carefully add steak and cook over high heat for 3 to 4 minutes, or until a golden-brown crust forms. Turn steak over and cook an additional 2 minutes.

4. Reduce heat to medium; add butter. Carefully tilt skillet slightly and spoon foamy butter over steak for 2 to 3 minutes, or to desired doneness. Transfer steak to a plate; cover loosely with foil and let rest for 5 minutes. Thinly slice steak against the grain.

5. To assemble sandwiches: Spread horseradish mayonnaise over cuts sides of rolls. Arrange lettuce on bottom halves of rolls; top each evenly with sliced steak, shredded Cheddar cheese and 1 tablespoon caramelized onions. Close with top halves of rolls.

Thanks so much for reading *A Country Wedding*. We hope you enjoyed it!

You might like these other books from Hallmark Publishing:

*Journey Back to Christmas*
*Christmas in Homestead*
*Love You Like Christmas*
*A Heavenly Christmas*
*A Dash of Love*
*Love Locks*
*The Perfect Catch*
*Like Cats and Dogs*
*Dater's Handbook*

For information about our new releases and exclusive offers, sign up for our free newsletter at hallmarkchannel.com/hallmark-publishing-newsletter

You can also connect with us here:

Facebook.com/HallmarkPublishing

Twitter.com/HallmarkPublish